Brightfellow

Brightfellow

A NOVEL

▬ RIKKI DUCORNET ▬

Coffee House Press
Minneapolis
2016

Coffee House Press books are available to the trade through our primary distributor, Consortium Book Sales & Distribution, cbsd.com or (800) 283-3572. For personal orders, catalogs, or other information, write to info@coffeehousepress.org.

Coffee House Press is a nonprofit literary publishing house. Support from private foundations, corporate giving programs, government programs, and generous individuals helps make the publication of our books possible. We gratefully acknowledge their support in detail in the back of this book.

Library of Congress Cataloging-in-Publication Data

Names: Ducornet, Rikki, 1943– author.
Title: Brightfellow / Rikki Ducornet.
Description: Minneapolis : Coffee House Press, 2016.
Identifiers: LCCN 2015037489 | ISBN 9781566894401 (paperback)
Subjects: | BISAC: FICTION / Literary. | FICTION / Psychological. |
    FICTION / Coming of Age. | FICTION / Romance / Gothic. |
    GSAFD: Bildungsromans.
Classification: LCC PS3554.U279 B75 2016 | DDC 813/.54—dc23
LC record available at http://lccn.loc.gov/2015037489

Acknowledgments

Part 1 of *Brightfellow* appeared in *Conjunctions 63: Speaking Volumes*, 2014. My thanks to Rick for the books, the ink; Linda for the pens, the walks in the woods.

Printed in the United States of America

23 22 21 20 19 18 17 16   1 2 3 4 5 6 7 8

For the Lannans, the month
at Marfa where this book
begins. For my son, his creative
spirit, his courage.

I was off and not a soul was aware. For it appeared to all that I was still among them, upon my little bed, rapt in child's play.

—Patti Smith, *Woolgathering*

Brightfellow

-ONE-

THE LINOLEUM SWELLS WITH STORIES. As he plays, darkness rises from the floor and slowly claims the room. Outside, a heavy rain falls and then it ends. Outside, the world spins, and he is the only one alone.

He cautiously steps from one island to the next. Cautiously! His feet are bare and small. Sometimes he considers them with curiosity. He doesn't know he's beautiful. He doesn't know he's lonely and that his fear is not of his making, that it will haunt him for the rest of his life. It will impede him years from now—twist and turn him just as an incessant wind twists and turns a tree—just as it will in unexpected ways nourish him. Yes: it will both nourish and impede him. And this is a terrible thing. How can he undo such a tangle?

The damage, already there, is subtle. As is its progress. It reaches for the future like smoke. The world bends beneath the weight of such malfeasance. There is a smell to it, a flavor and a mood, a familiar weather. Although he is six, only—six!—he is accustomed to it. It is the atmosphere that sustains his tirelessly imagining mind. Oh! How tirelessly he dreams! He cannot know it, but already he yearns to live richly. That is to say deeply and with excitement. He is thirsty but it does not occur to him to drink.

To begin: it is late in the day. Early evening. And he is alone. He is a good child, far too good for his own safety. The house is in shadow, the woods beyond in shadow, and behind his door, the familiar rooms all are in shadow. One day the word *penumbra* will appeal to him. But he is too small now to know it. He plays at explorer. It is his way of claiming and knowing those charmed islands that burn so brightly in his mind. *Here,* he says, his head tilted to one side, *are antelopes.* (*Antelope*—a word he loves.) *Parrots in the trees.* Parrots with beaks made to crack nuts, and with wings strong enough to master hurricanes. He draws a breath, and crossing over to the next island, the island of elephants, blows it out. Trumpeting elephants, their toes fused together. And snakes! Even more beautiful than the garter snakes that live in the backyard where the sumac grows. More beautiful than the copperheads that rule the woods where he walks sweeping the paths with a stick just as if they were planted with explosives. Poised on one foot he says: *Be careful.* Again he dares confront the linoleum's treacherous waters. *Giraffes,* he nods, greeting them, coming to rest. Solidly planted and still, he looks at the world around him. The islands are all alike, gold-colored blossoms floating on an indigo sea. Volcanic islands with lakes, caves, quicksand. How he loves these islands! These epic journeys!

There is an archipelago that begins under his bed and goes all the way to his door. It shines with beauty and danger. There are flowers that have voices and sing to children. There is a poisonous toad that speaks in riddles, and the wrong sort of snake, thick as a chimney, concealed in the dappled light. Beyond the door is the bathroom he needs to visit but dares not, as well as the kitchen, his parents' mysterious bedroom (a place of disquiet), the living room, the small dining room where he likes to draw pictures because the table is so big his crayons can't roll all the way to the edge and fall to the floor. Crayons, he thinks, are like baby snakes in *rigor mortis* (his mother's words).

But the linoleum. It's risky. If he continues this way, naming the mountains and the animals, he might wander *too far*, might not find his way home. The sea is black, the islands dimmer by the second. The yard outside, every room in the house, have surrendered to a night lit, but barely, by a moon broken in half.

Island by island he must step to the light switch and turn it on, but it's so dark he can barely see where he is going. He might take a wrong turn and tumble onto a star headed for Mars. He really needs to pull himself together now and make his way to the light switch. And the bathroom after.

A car passes, briefly filling the room with light. The light is like an eye searching him out. But he has been good, hasn't he? There is no reason to be afraid. The switch is within reach when he stumbles and with a cry falls to his knees. He touches the floor. Dry land!

A door slams, his mother's voice calls his name. When he reaches the light the first thing he sees is the door's little brass head. He thinks that the doorknob must be the door's head even if it is in a funny place. And it has his face.

Sometimes when he is alone in the house he hears voices, her voice, so he is not certain it is her voice now. Or if the steps coming down the hall toward him are hers. Or who she will be, his mother or the one he dare not name. "Stub?" she calls out from the hallway, "Stub?" The little face on the door turns; he watches it turning and she's there, his mother, bending to hug him, saying: *Poor little fellow in the dark, dark house all alone!*

—

She dispels the shadows, all of them; it is astonishing, the radical shift that takes place: the world is *back on track*—a thing she likes to say. *Back on track* for now and maybe forever. And there will be Chinese noodles. The boxes are on the kitchen counter, and a hard head of lettuce, the sharp kitchen knife, the green and white crockery from Mexico. When she's in a good mood she says: *Let's put some crunchy crackers on the crockery and chow down.* And he will laugh; he will be one with laughter. If you could peel him like an orange you would find laughter all the way through. (This is how it should be; why isn't it always like this? Chinese noodles and crackers and crockery and caresses and laughter from the top of his head to the tips of his toes.)

She is so beautiful he wishes he could scramble onto her lap, but she's leaning over the kitchen table with the green and white dishes painted with leaves, so round and pretty they make him glad, like a cat that has had its milk.

Or a tree in the early morning full of singing birds. This is what her magic does to him, her white magic.

His mother has a radio show. It is strange and maybe wonderful how she fits inside the little brown box. His mother, her square face, her round bottom, her funny hair, her wool suit, her high-heeled shoes, her entire brain and voice, her tongue and teeth, her laughter and her shouting—it all fits in there like a slice of bread in a toaster.

There is a thing he knows: food made with love is hot. Scorching when it went into the white paper boxes, the food is *still hot*. Tonight his mother is a good fairy, her eyes sparkling behind her glasses. She looks nice and talks easily about the mysterious world she visits when she is across the river in Kahontsi. He relishes time with her. In the morning she will leave for work dressed in tweed. A silly word like *Tweedledee*. When he thinks of tweed, he imagines his mother going to Kahontsi on roller skates. But instead, off she bustles in her little leather pumps, her frizzed hair tight on her head, makeup served upon her face like a fried egg on a plate, and he is overcome with admiration and disdain.

Her face is much better in the morning before she paints it. There are little creases beside her blue eyes and a blue mole on her upper lip. Her skin is soft, not sticky. Saturday and Sunday she is lazy; the mornings unspool languorously. The house smells of coffee. When his father is home it smells of bacon and eggs and French toast, and Stub doesn't notice that the linoleum shuts down and stays that way, its secret life silenced. Silenced, too, her sudden anger that pummels him like a black rain.

His father has never raised a hand to him, nor his voice. Once, only once, he lost his temper, and ran after Stub to punish him. But Stub ran faster and his father, a heavy smoker, stopped in his tracks, panting, empty of anger, sucking on air and laughing. Then they were both flat on their backs laughing together. Rolling around on the grass *like caterpillars,* said Stub.

It never occurs to Stub that his father does not know that sometimes his mother shakes him so violently his teeth rattle like marbles and his heart thrashes like a fish in a bowl of ink. That there is a bad mother, a good mother—like a planet and its moon spinning together, rising and falling, the one eclipsing the other. He knows his father will never purposefully hurt him, knows this in his bones, and then there is this other thing: the family. The shape, whole and good, they make together. Whole and good but also bad, a world of shadows, danger at its heart.

Always his father comes home late, and even if Stub is fast asleep, he strides into his room easily, islands and oceans falling away, he might as well be levitating, floats to the bed, kisses Stub on the cheek. This kiss floods the moment with promises Stub knows his father intends to keep.

Once his mother said to him: *You sleep with your mouth open, your hands crossed over your chest like a corpse!* He sleeps *like a corpse stiff as a snake in rigor mortis.*

Sometimes when she turns on the radio to hear her own voice he resents it.

Sometimes when the snow falls she says: *How I love weather.* And he loves her for it. Loves her so much his heart blooms like a tiger lily and he roars his happiness; he roars and runs about and his pleasure delights her. In these moments their friendship is secure, eternal, luminous; their friendship rings the hours. These words of hers give him hope; he, too, loves weather, the safety of seasons, each bringing a gift: snow, rain, sun, wind. But because he is a dreamy child, fall is his favorite. Perhaps it reflects the best moments of family life: days of color, of clement weather—and this before the first mornings of heavy fog; the first blizzard when the sky is wiped away and the sun dissolves in brine; the first ice storm, one of many, when he can hear the world outside shattering.

If he looks like a corpse when he sleeps, does this mean he will die in his sleep? Sometimes he pokes his gums with a pencil to make them hurt, to make them bleed.

—

Someone is coming to live with them. This way he will never be alone again in the evenings. When the bus brings him home, Jenny will be there to look after him. She was living in the madhouse, the one off the highway just a few miles away. The madhouse where people who are *on their way to health and feeling better* sit on the front porch in rocking chairs watching the cars go by. He has seen them rocking back and forth. Perhaps he has seen Jenny on the porch from the school bus window, rocking and sniffling and thinking, or chewing gum or smoking. Is she thick, ugly, and sad? He once saw a lady who had hair like dead mice glued to her head. And another one, *all nerve and bone* (his mother's words) with a great red nose sticking out of her face like a swollen toe. No, says his mother. Jenny is pretty, thin as a pencil with hair like yellow string. Tonight when his father comes home he will bring Jenny with him. She will live in the spare room. She will stay in the spare room, not wander, except when invited elsewhere, such as the kitchen, or when they are alone together, playing in his room. And she will cook for him. During the day when he is at school, Jenny will be at work washing dishes. He wonders if she will make sandwiches. She will. And macaroni. Meatloaf. All the things he likes. Will she tell him stories? She will. Where does she go to wash dishes? Annie's. Up the way. Jenny likes to put her hands into hot soapy water. Soapy water is what she likes better than anything. When she comes to live with them, she will wash her hands over and over and Stub will fall asleep to the sound. Jenny's hands thick with suds like sheep's wool; he will lie in bed listening. Clocks will dissolve and the passage of time will take on the shape of a heart. Stub will think: *That is the sound of sweet Jenny washing her hands. She is on the mend but she is still crazy, sort of.* And this is how we know: the suds filling the sink night after night like lambs.

Here is how Stub dreams of Jenny:

He dreams that she is shearing wool and that the wool accumulates around her in drifts like snow. When his mother's voice hatchets into the room and he awakens, he knows that he has glimpsed something both true and mysterious.

He dreams again. Of Jenny standing in the foam of the ocean; it froths like boiling milk. She has a cup in her hand made of silver; it's Stub's cup, the one he had as a baby. Jenny dips it into the foaming sea and offers it to him. It tastes like milk sweetened with honey. When Stub awakens, every hour of that day is diaphanous.

One afternoon when Stub has returned from school and the orange bus has vanished behind the hill, and he is in the kitchen with Jenny eating gingersnaps, he hears his mother's voice on the radio and puts his hands over his ears. We can turn it off, Jenny says, and she does. The delicious aroma of subversion fills the room, and Stub radiates within a cool plume of light. How easy, he realizes, to shut the box off! That day something happens that greatly matters, something good but also dangerous. And funny. When Jenny turns the knob and he laughs out loud, she joins in.

Later she asks to see the book he loves best. He brings her *Little Black Sambo Lost at Sea*. A beautiful book packed with pictures and thick, black letters. Jenny loves letters.

She says that when they collide into one another they are like animals that change shape before your eyes. They leave tracks across the page. They are round, soft, thorny; they have edges. The letters come together, she whispers right into his ear, in order to delight, to derange us. They come together, they hold hands, they caress, they bruise one another, they *force the soul down deeper,* they make us thirsty for unimaginable things, they shake their limbs and dance, the page is their stage, they make music, see: that *h* looks like a harp.

"Is it true," Stub whispers into *her* ear, "that they burned a hole into your head?"

"Yes." She whispers back. "There was an *intruder,* a poet, I think, sitting inside my head *on her very own chair*! So . . . someone thought to . . . someone thought to . . . look!" And she points to another letter, like a person, wanting to say hello.

Little Black Sambo is sitting on a big box of oranges floating in the middle of the sea. "O!" he says. "Good thing I'm sitting on this box of oranges!" If you close your eyes, Jenny says, leaning closer, and think about that letter *O*, you can smell the rind and see the seeds inside. The box is tied with string, which is why it has an *X*. And see the nice, mouthy *O* in the middle. Big enough to swallow an orange. Skin and all. A good word, *box*. It has so much room inside.

When in the mornings the school bus comes, Jenny is there to say good-bye. She squeezes his hand; hers is long and cool and friendly. Her fingers are very clean, cleaner than anyone else's. And soft. They smell of almonds. Her eyes are green and strange, flecked with gold dust and cacao. Her hair floats around her face like yellow string, just as his mother said. Jenny is beautiful, dressed for work in sneakers and a gray cotton dress. She wears a brown wool cardigan because the day is *nippy*. She says: When you get back I'll be here. To be here always is my intention.

In school when his teacher asks he tells her: Mommy is in the radio and Daddy sells seeds. He goes to people's houses *door to door*. Flowers, he tells her: marigolds and pansies (which means "thinking of you" in France). Vetegebles, too. *Vegetables*, she corrects him. He says: Radishes. Pink ones, red and white. Even black ones. I've never heard of black radishes, she says. Tell your daddy I'd like to buy a package of those black radish seeds.

—

This is a day unfolding unlike any other. The sensation of Jenny's hand in his own and his teacher's interest in his father's radishes. Then in the afternoon when the bus stops beside the path that leads to his house, Jenny is out front feeding crackers to the ants that live *everywhere. Not just under the front porch*. Ants, she tells him, like a parade. Ants, she continues, have built a city under the porch, a fantastic city of sand with towers and pyramids and map rooms and museums. They live in the dark; ants have noses for eyes. They sleep under the best smooth stones. There are corridors, more than anyone can count; ants *don't* have doorknobs. They fear anteaters. Ant-eating birds. Little boys who do cruel things with mirrors. Understand, she says, that this is a warning. He assures her he loves the ants, too.

At the center of the ants' city, there is a park and a long table set for community suppers. The plates are made of toenail trimmings people have left unattended on the bathroom floor; the ants go into the house just as soon as people leave to look for them. They look for the things people have abandoned in corners, under the living room couch, behind the crockery, in the breadbox, between the pages of books, in the deep creases of the upholstered rocker, in his father's sock drawer—*My father's sock drawer!* Stub explodes with laughter. And the pantry. Jenny picks up a twig and pushes it around in the grass. Above all, the pantry! Grain by grain they make off with the sugar, the flour, the honey grahams and gingersnaps, the lost buttons. Lost buttons? Yes. A button is a fantastic weapon when you are an ant. When the ants go to war it might look like a game of tiddlywinks to you and me, but a button sent flying into an anteater's eye will send it packing, let me tell you.

There are islands in my room, Stub tells Jenny. Would you like to see them?

—

That weekend his father comes home. He carries a small false-leather suitcase for his shirts and underwear and an orange leather valise with brass bumpers and tacks. Inside, packages of seeds are tucked in careful rows. To see the valise open *stuns the senses* (Jenny). Who could have known how beautiful packages of seeds could be? Even the radishes are a revelation. The purple beets look like people, Jenny says, all tummy with leaves. Things from another, newer world. Somewhere, she decides, vegetables are as prized as rubies. Somewhere people make ruby soup and rings out of radishes.

He can see that Jenny makes his father uncomfortable. Night settles in. Jenny eats a sandwich in her room. Then, even as they are still at supper, she starts sudsing her hands.

That night he dreams of ants overtaking the house. They get into the radio and walk off with his mother's voice. Outside, the air is thick and fast with fistfuls of greasy snow. The following evening his father is stuck upstate and his mother stranded in Kahontsi. *Stranded* is sweet sugar on the tongue. He imagines his mother standing alone in a cold room looking out the window with a frown on her face. Fully dressed in her winter coat, muff, fur hat, fur-lined boots and gloves—she has run out of things to say and she is frowning. Wires are down, the streets are still, and Jenny makes rice. They spend the next day at the kitchen table building houses out of stiff paper, held together with tape and glue. A hardware store, a barbershop, a post office, a firehouse, and a water tower. Jenny makes bologna sandwiches with tender Wonder Bread and pungent mustard, and after lunch they build a bell tower because a town needs a bell in case of emergencies. Emergencies, they make a list, consist of: fires, enemy attacks, meteors, people running amok. Wolves can overtake a place and so can outlaws. We need a cemetery, says Jenny. A bakery, says Stub, with pies in the window. They build a water tower with legs made of pencils that refuses to stand up. This water tower, says Jenny, has a mind all its own. I'm putting cracker crumbs in the bakery, says Stub, to make sure the ants come by to check this all out.

Jenny proposes: a hotel for insomniacs. An observatory from which to consider the question: just what sort of cheese *is* the moon made of? A river that spills all of the world's anger into a pool where everything sighs.

That night they sleep together like brother and sister. The snow keeps on coming and in the morning there is so much of it banked up against the front door they can't open it. They eat bologna and rice pudding and spend the day making a library stacked with important books for elephants: *The Nature of Trumpeting. How to Protect Your Assets.* She figures out a way to keep the water tower from falling over. When the telephone rings they are in the thick of it and cannot, do not, answer. Jenny says: That will be your mother. Stub says: I'd like pygmies to live in this village. We'll make a jungle, says Jenny. And put the village smack in the middle. That way they can play all day in the jungle and come home at night and eat pie.

Jenny turns up the thermostat. She cleans the house. The bathroom is spotless, the linoleum in Stub's room has been scrubbed and rinsed many times over and then waxed to a *high shine.* Words you can say breathing in and out: breathe in: *high;* breathe out: *shine.* A magical incantation. Jenny and Stub breathe together, stepping from island to island on the sparkling linoleum. Can you, he asks, hear the elephants? Yes. And I can already see them, swimming light as bubbles. Looking at their legs the fish think they are dead heads. Fish have very short memories. If an injustice is done to them, they forget all about it. You can hook a fish over and over. Its mouth bleeds and it wonders why. If you hook it, gut it, clean it, cook it, eat it, digest it, shit it—it will not remember. But elephants remember everything. Just like we do.

Late afternoon. Outside the white witches of the air are busy packing up their needles and bits of unfinished tatting. Mother is trapped in Kahontsi, Stub says. Trapped in Kahontsi, Jenny agrees. Trapped in a teepee! Jenny dares. Trapped in a teepee! laughs Stub. The phone rings and rings and then it stops.

Jenny fetches a book from her room. By Verner Vanderloon, an old man who lives in seclusion somewhere by the river. A book with pictures as strange as the strangest thing you can think of. A small book bound in green leather, almost black, with silver letters pressed into the cover. Stub rubs a finger over them and with Jenny's help reads: *Ancient Roots and Ways.* I stole it, Jenny whispers, from the Half Way House. She explains that the Half Way House is where she was when she was halfway here, on her way, although she didn't know it yet, to him, to Stub. Now, now, she says, putting her arm around him when she sees the familiar troubled look on his face, I've *always* been halfway here, you know? Until I got here! Look at this!

Jenny opens the book and there is a picture of the skulls of apes: baboon, orangutan, gorilla, chimpanzee. She reads the names aloud to him. From that moment on he cannot look at the letter *B* without seeing the skull of a baboon. Jenny turns the page and together they look at the skulls of men from long ago, before they were people, when they were only *halfway here.*

You know, Jenny tells him, we still have our monkey ways.

The next day the sun is shining and the snow truck elbows past. There is a deep white road where minutes before there was none. A deep white road like the one his father is taking south, his winter hat on his head and his beautiful valise beside him. His mother, too, is traveling. On roller skates with wheels spinning so fast they are invisible. His mother tears down the white road in her tweeds all the way from Kahontsi across the frozen river carrying her lipstick and her keys, a brown paper bag with a fresh package of margarine, one blood-red spot smack in the middle, her hair fried and stuck to her head. Or maybe she will breeze in with hot Chinese noodles and a story she will tell them breathlessly, happy as a lark. Or she'll come in angry, steaming, shouting: *Why didn't you answer the phone?* And smack Stub, and smack Jenny, and Jenny will break apart and all her pretty pins and springs will spill out across the floor and that will be that.

Ever after he will wonder: *Why was Jenny sent away?* Two years later his mother, too, disappears, wanting *more of the world, more of life.* And there they are, Stub and his dad, sitting in silence face to face, the favorite green and white dishes scowling and cold to the touch, the linoleum purged of magic and Stub breaking the silence with another nagging question, the *only* question: *Why can't we bring Jenny home?* Because of another mouth to feed, Jenny's mouth a big hungry *O* eating the orange, seeds and all. Besides, no one knows where she's gone. Kahontsi, maybe.

"Not Kahontsi."

"Maybe Ohneka, then."

"People don't just disappear."

"They do. All the time."

His dad's valise replaced by a box of plumbing tools. *Lonely work. Sometimes it's hard to persevere.* (His father's words.)

-TWO-

A LONG THE HUDSON RIVER, the world goes on forever, unspooling, and just when you think you know it, something happens, the summer is snatched away by an ice storm, a blizzard dissolves the spring, there are moths in sudden numbers, an unprecedented migration of geese. Autumn arrives unparalleled in its beauty. The river gleams, there are shad and snapping turtles, quantities of water chestnuts, and under porches: copperheads.

If America has gods, this is where they dwell—under rocks, in the branches of trees, in ivy, skunkweed, the hearts of fish, the flight of geese. But—everyone says it—things no longer shine as they once did. Ever since the war, everything is dimmer.

When he was very little he knew—if only for a brief moment—that the world was imbued with light. That he came into the world beaming and burning. He was always combusting. He was enchanted.

Here is a curious paradox: he is a man, quick as a whip, thin as a razor, by acts of will invisible, someone who snakes about, who is always needing (ah! This pesky *need* of his!) to puzzle the world back together again, to polish the pieces and make them shine. But as he was undone so early he cannot know—no matter how avidly he watches the lives around him unfold—where *his pieces go*, and this despite his desperate, his imperious need to gather the pieces together (and he is *tireless*), to see it all fall into place.

He grew up three miles down the road from the campus, in a place so small it was known by the name of its one bar: Annie's. When he was growing up and a kid asked him where he lived, he'd say *up the road from Annie's.* If they had not heard of Annie's he'd say *'bout four miles east of town.* Meaning Hawkskill, where the school was, the post office and dry-goods store—all that—and the hotel-restaurant that still fills up when folks drop their kids off, turn up for Christmas break, Easter, graduation. For this reason Hawkskill is called a college town, although there is not much there to attract students. The rest of the time the hotel clients are traveling salesmen, and in cider season, on the long weekend of the county fair, tourists.

When he was a boy, and this happened a year or two after his mother left, his father took him and his grandmother out for a big midday meal to celebrate his grandmother's birthday. She had turned eighty and they ate roast beef and gravy with Yorkshire pudding and mashed potatoes. His father, usually taciturn, talked about what he'd seen and been bewildered by on the campus—students kissing in public, even mixed couples; he disliked the girls' wild hair. Their bare feet and thighs. Their untamed, their graceful ways. *Shameless,* he complained. But the day he saw a kid playing a fiddle on the commons, playing it well, he thought it was tremendous.

—

When Stub turns nine, he decides to check out the campus for himself. Near summer's end, he walks the three miles and finds it deserted. He wanders freely, enthralled by the expansive beauty of the place, the inscrutable stone buildings, the ink of their shadows, the impossible grass curving toward a forested horizon. Lying down in a saucer of grass beside a flagpole, its flag, too, at rest, he thinks he could haunt this place, move along the many dark recesses beneath the walls and plantings and not be seen. Somewhere a clock chimes the hour and he looks up at the sky and thinks that everything he learns must be put to good use.

In front of the library he comes upon kids his own age, *faculty brats* (his dad's words), he supposes, playing kick the can. The can has been kicked, and as they scatter they look at him with disdain—or so he thinks—and dash away with a piece of him. He feels ashamed, somehow. Corroded. But the library is open, and bravely he walks in. As he passes the front desk the librarian welcomes him, standing up from his chair, which doesn't make him any taller. "I am so pleased you have come in," he says, "you're the first person I've seen all day. But I haven't seen you before."

"My dad works here," Stub tells him. "Fixing things."

"What's his name? Perhaps I've met him."

"Jiggs Wiznet," Stub tells him. "I'm Stub."

"I know Jiggs Wiznet!" the librarian exclaims. "He fixed the library toilets and he did a nice job. It makes good sense you both share the same last name. I'm Axel." As he speaks he scribbles something on a small square of stiff paper that turns out to be a library card. "If I were named Stub Wiznet, well . . . it would be perfect. I'm the dwarf, after all." He sighs softly. "Want to trade?"

"A dwarf?"

"Our time here is so brief—one day you'll see what I mean—and it would be better to have a perfect name." He hands Stub a card. "If I were a wrestler, well . . . Axel would do me fine. Are you wanting anything in particular? The card means you can take books home."

"Verner Vanderloon," Stub says, surprising himself. "I'd like a book of his."

"A book of Loon's! I knew Loon. A recluse. No one has seen him in years." He walks with Stub to the stacks. "We also have much of his library—a gift—in storage . . . no room left in the stacks." And then Stub is alone among more books than he imagined possible, Vanderloon's eight volumes, all with the familiar green leather bindings, tightly shelved together side by side within an ocean of books. The first thing he does is sit down on the floor and look at the spines. At that moment he vividly recalls Jenny and is freshly stricken by an old suffering.

At some point it occurs to him that he could live in the library. He could read all day and sleep on the floor at night.

Use the restrooms, and nobody would be the wiser. And when he got hungry he could steal a pie from the window-sill and run into the woods and eat his supper under the trees, among the ants, just as the animals do.

Terrible things happen all the time, he thinks, but not today. Terrible things, beautiful things, things of such power, of such bewilderment, lucent and dark as tar. But right now the universe, restless beyond imagining, a universe of rock and flame, whose nature is incandescence—a universe that flickers, its impatient forms blinking like fireflies in the night—astounds and delights him. Because he has in his hands a book of Vanderloon's, its text scattered with peculiar sketches like the scrawl of restless spiders. Sketches of altars exhaling smoke, of volcanoes spitting gravel and sparks, of pearl divers and temple gates, of naked people wielding clubs, their faces lifted, stunned by the sign of a meteor.

That night when Stub and his father are at supper, Stub remembers with nostalgia the family lunch they'd had in town not long before his grandmother passed. He asks if they could go again. His father says no, not ever, because the people in there make a man feel like a rag, like a rope of tripe. But Stub's memory is radically different. The waitress had been friendly and she had playfully mussed his hair. She had wrapped a fresh piece of pie in a shiny piece of foil for him to take home. Later on when Stub considers his childhood, that simple gesture will be one of the most benevolent instances he can retrieve.

Stub returns to the library often. Axel is always there for him, eager to talk, as he makes his way, doggedly, through Vanderloon's books: *Ancient Roots and Ways; Big Ears, Small Ears: Easter Island at War; Rules of Rage; Cannibal Ways; The Lost Archipelago; Primates in Paradise; Dream's Dying.* Axel advises: "Don't let Loon get you down, Stub. It's a dark vision." He continues:

"However much
The trunk be mangled, with the limbs lopped off,
The soul withdrawn and taken from the limbs,
Still lives the trunk and draws the vital air.
Lucretius," he says.

Stub cannot tell his father about Axel, Vanderloon, the library. Jiggs both resents the campus and fiercely protects his place in it. When Stub attempts to describe his first afternoon there, it is exactly as if he has unknowingly breached a taboo, desecrated the holy of holies. At home his isolation deepens. But instead of dying, his affections are displaced.

—

When Jiggs Wiznet falls apart, conquered by his frayed nerves, his injurious nights, his dromedary days, his fatal dawns—Stub has long split. He has claimed the campus for himself, knows it intimately. He is pragmatic and a thief. He has mastered the art of invisibility.

His first summer alone he bathes in the river, catches shad, builds fires. He sleeps in duck blinds, under a canoe, in an abandoned truck, graduates to the gym and showers there, uncovers an inexhaustible supply of soap. In the full heat of August he sleeps in the Dean's formal garden, under the Founder's Oak, on a purloined blanket. (The dorms are bountiful!) That winter he takes up residence in a spacious cabinet beneath the biology lab's collection of bottled anomalies—a room rarely entered. The following summer he moves to the Utilities House, appreciates its homey smell of dust and lamp oil. He beds down in an expensive sleeping bag on the impressively thick and level floor, his few necessities stashed under the sink. The closet provides a wealth of paper towels and a pair of galoshes. Not much is locked, but when necessary he proves a master at rotating cams, knows how to stack them much as planets and their sun stack up during an eclipse. In this way the years pass. He is a recluse, a scholar. He is a dissembler. When in a tight spot, he invents identities. He is strange.

The fall Stub turns nineteen he claims the library's abandoned storage room—the very place where Vanderloon's personal library is stowed away. Here he builds himself a den within a maze of books. A scholar during the day, he roams the stacks, reads, takes notes in recesses provided with desks and ink. He finds a pen with a tip that appears to be made of gold. Dressed in preppy discards harvested from the dorms, he is inconspicuous. He watches the world around him unseen. A year passes. A child catches his attention. She appears often, suddenly, without warning—up a tree, on a roof, dashing across a lawn. Resplendent, she stands out among the faculty brats. Safely housed in the library, time on his hands, Stub begins a journal:

The library space, if airless, is an oasis of privacy and peace. I have my reading lamp. It's toasty. The toilet, pristine; the sink, ever ready for my little rituals. (A vagrant, I go about my days clean as a whistle.) Sometimes I think that had it all started out differently, I might have taken the world by storm rather than exhausting myself slinking about, purloining soap and other people's galoshes. Yet I seem to have been born with a special instinct; it is amazing how instinctive this existence is if one is to be successful. Yet I often wonder—where does this invisibility lead me? What guides it? Whence the source of my impassioned scholarship (Vanderloon!) and, above all, impassioned interest in a little girl (and she is beautiful) named Asthma? What stars have marked us? What tropes of the blood?

Then again . . . what is wonderful about this life—as sordid as it might appear (and it is *sordid! How I long for a loving touch! An admiring glance! A word of encouragement!)—is the way the proximate world unfolds for me: it is* mine. *There is not a single nook or cranny on this campus and its environs (the graveyard, athletic fields, studios, theater, laboratories, classrooms, kitchens, dorms, staff and faculty housing, etc., etc.) I have not managed at sometime or another to scrutinize. (On moonless nights I move about as swiftly, as silently as a bat.)*

I have wintered in the safety of the biology lab's hospitable cabinet, its lowest shelf as deep as a coffin and ceiling twice as high (the lab sinks are big enough to soak in!). I have wintered in the mop room of the kitchen and with discretion supped on cans stacked there with seeming boundlessness. (Who could miss two months' worth of cans abused in such a clever way that only eight cans [each lasting a week] are consumed: pork and beans, ravioli, clam chowder, minestrone, chicken noodle, tomato bisque, green pea, chicken gumbo.) Meals augmented by calculated visits to the faculty wives' kitchens, always abounding in cottage cheese, cheddar cheese, sliced ham. And always in the cellar pantries: French pickles, homemade jam, seasonal apples. If one is clever, things vanish in such a way as to inspire no more than a brief moment of perplexity. This said (I admit to this; I am, after all, no enigma to myself!), I live by the seat of my pants.

Last summer, when all the families on Faculty Circle had walked over to the Dean's house to watch the fireworks, I slipped into a kitchen and feasted on what remained of a Fourth of July supper, the few ribs sweet and sticky; I was nearly overcome by the taste, the slaw swimming in the bottom of the Danish bowl, the rolls in their basket, the butter in its dish. I feasted secure in the knowledge that they, in their affluence, swept along in the bustle and comforts of family life heightened by a national holiday, would never notice a few ribs reduced to bone, the salad bowl licked clean.

I am, as are all men: mindful, artful, perceptive, creative—and an animal. Determined to survive, to sleep in safety and not go hungry. I imagine that my chosen life says something about other men, about man's nature. And that in spite of all these digressions I am leaning toward greater things. Capable of greatness. What if my life is not only the mirror of my own thwarted destiny, or the mirror of mankind's thwarted destiny, but the mirror of my species's capacity to overcome the worst odds? The odds of a collapsed infancy in a world shuddering with sadness. (It is true I could be doing better than counting cans of minestrone and bathing in sinks that reek of formaldehyde. I acknowledge this freely.) But back to the moment. As I return to my current den, drawn as are the fish by starlight, my path is illumed by the stars and the moon. The night sky has a child's color; it is the color of her hair . . . the twilight is the color of her eyes, the earth is the color of her mood, and I can hear her almost-imperceptible wheezing in the breeze; her perfume is the perfume caught among the thorns of the blackberry bushes that line the path. And I think as I approach the Night Library that she is all things to me: star, astral light, perfume of bramble, moonlight, and secrecy: life itself. Asthma.

When asked, which happens from time to time, I say I am researching Verner Vanderloon and, come to think of it, this is true. After all, his papers are here along with the books, and I am deep into all of it. (Read some Malinowski! *Axel admonished me before his death.* Read some Lévi-Strauss, some Boas! Read Margaret Mead! *But I have a mind to finish what I have begun; such an interesting mind, Loon's!) If asked (this has never happened) there is much I can say about him, his intimate and groundbreaking work (his* obsession *Axel said) with human cruelty, the connections he makes (considered by his peers illadvised) between man's terror and resentment of mortality, and his paradoxical impulse to take death's side, to extinguish promiscuous wives (one example) who he imagines, in one of his most charming digressions, being revered on another planet for all they do for the public good, arousing feelings of conviviality, good cheer, fraternity—not to mention inspiring the erotic fires of* all *the wives. (His chapter on the Temple Whores of Tantric India could not be more wistful.) Yet his detractors call him* the dog who always barks up the wrong tree.

There is, admittedly, some weird stuff about the name of God and Vanderloon's inquiries into the origins of self-awareness. My own, *he writes,* was awakened by the sound of my grandmother's garter pistol going off, not by accident, and shattering my granddad's ribs.

Vanderloon's research into the many forms marriage takes miraculously coincides with the ways in which the gods conspire and interfere with family life. What comes to mind is the familial traditions of the Episcopate Islands of the Eastern Rim, in which the eldest brother deflowers his sisters, who then defer to him in all things, including the vocabulary they are to use for the rest of their lives, the time of day they may speak, and the subjects of their discourse—such as the migrations of lizards, the color of edible moth pupae, the (limited) ways in which the backs of chairs may be decorated. On another island the bride is made to name the groom's every family member and ancestor but forget her own; on yet another the bride in coitus cuts off her groom's left ear, which she then gives to her mother-in-law as proof of her undying fealty.

Vanderloon also darkly rejoices in stories of mothers tossing mush at their infants' faces; it must learn to swallow what it can of the mush and *its pride simultaneously. "Our species is doomed* to perish cursing its own boundless absurdity," Vanderloon is said to have asserted when asked to speak at his retirement supper.

Back to Asthma. She is eight, the very age I was when Mother vanished into the box forever and Father, once so kind, began to devolve into debility and viciousness. Little Asthma! As mine was, her mother, Blackie, is a screamer. Asthma. A name that is soft on the tongue, that, like cotton candy, dissolves. My own fairy child. One day I hope to know her as well as I know Vanderloon's books, the way I know every pop and snap the library makes in the dark after hours and the taste of canned minestrone when you have spooned it into your mouth for twenty consecutive days. (I believe I am the only person on the planet who knows just what this tastes like.) If I could, I would count every hair on Asthma's head, and not just to know their number, mind you, but to uncover that number's precise meaning, cabalistically if you will—in terms not of God's name or the numbers of hairs He had on his head or chin (a childish exercise), but of how that number coincides with the scattered pieces of the world as they couple and uncouple ceaselessly: there is a pattern to all this, only it is invisible, and furthermore it takes a particular frame of mind, and it takes time (!), it takes intention (!), to see it. Asthma. I hear Blackie scream and think: Go in peace, my little bell, my little snail, my little seaside pail; Asthma the salt, the surf of my soul.

Deep in the dark days of winter, I think: How good is the summer! I can get around joyfully and tirelessly, live in comfort *in the Utilities House, its windows open to the breeze, and much like a cartoon character, snag a pie from a windowsill (or a kitchen table) and in the dark of night, make off with the plump promise of a refrigerated chicken!*

One of the fine things about campus life is that intellectuals (well, maybe this isn't true of French intellectuals) are not into dogs, and if they are, it's not a watchdog but a child-friendly dog, a sleepy dog with floppy ears and droopy jowls, a cat-friendly dog. A dog that will protect the parakeet from the cat. Parakeets are popular and as long as I don't collide into a cage in the dark (this learned the hard way) don't set off any alarms. For one thing, they appear to be much like chickens; as long as they are in the dark they sleep a deep and dreamless sleep. (The one time I collided into a cage it belonged to a large gray parrot who roused the house with the word: Parcheesi! *[It turned out that was its name.] Like an adulterer I had to hide behind the sofa until everything settled down. Parrots, I have noticed, are popular with narcissists.)*

—

When the faculty brats play in the forest that unfolds behind the Circle, their shouts are shuttled by the trees. Decomposing trunks bridge the moon. Being the children of professors, their dragons guard golden apples. They play at pharaohs, the collapse of Thebes. They know something of the great plague. Sometimes the games they play are dangerous, as when Asthma spends a long afternoon tied to a tree. Lost among the seething wars of starships deeper in the woods, the boys forget her, abandon her for the river's rocky beaches and then, at day's end, the comfort of the Indian Wars at home, televised in black and white.

The curious thing about Asthma is that she is not afraid. Her captivity provides an occasion to ponder a number of beauties, paradoxes, and contradictions. Overhead, several thousand geese row the air. Almost imperceptible, a fox, terrible and wonderful, slips past with a rabbit in its mouth. The two animals stain the air with a scent of appetite and fear that lingers for hours. And Asthma sees a copperhead uncoil and spill from under a fallen tree, mossy and hectic with the comings and goings of beetles the size of thumbs. *What*, she wonders, *what on earth can they be thinking?*

Asthma has seen copperheads before—the woods are alive with them; the children walk with sticks, thrashing their way through everything, underbrush, bramble, high grass, sumac, and cattails. They rejoice whenever they see a snake because they thrive on risk (one will become a pilot, one a stockbroker, one a gambler, and one a suicide)—enfevered when they see a hornet nest hanging above them like a severed head or whenever they see something dead. Tied to her tree, Asthma remains composed as the afternoon submits to evening—composed because her mind is gorged with fairy tales and she knows something miraculous will happen. Which at last it does, when the boys, smelling of piss and clay, and looking frightened and hurried, brandish their pocketknives and cut her free as she glowers. She may only be eight, but she twists this way and that in a manner she knows is provocative. And when Roland—her favorite—dares look her in the eyes and stutter an apology, she coyly turns her head away in a gesture both studied and rehearsed. (Asthma has seen how Blackie does this very thing when her playmates' fathers provoke her with *their* eyes.)

How strange the world is! How full of marvels! On her way home Asthma passes Professor Brunelleschi, who is on his way to the cemetery where his wife is buried. Asthma's own room overlooks it, so she is well aware of his clockwork consistency.

Asthma likes the cemetery. For one thing, it is practically an extension of her own house. The backyard gives way to lilac bushes, boulders, and brambles, and the next thing you know, you are standing on the cemetery path in the company of songbirds, squirrels, skippers, and painted ladies. Coffins blanketed in sod.

She is careful not to disturb Professor Brunelleschi while he is speaking to his dead wife. Asthma fondly remembers Noni Brunelleschi, who had been golden as if glazed and who had smelled of her husband's Turkish tobacco. Noni, so soft and round—except for her piano playing, which was *fortissimo!* and angular.

"*Bellezza ed onestate,*" he murmurs. "I am no longer witty. I no longer laugh."

Asthma likes the dead. They are unobtrusive. One can dream beside them without disruption. Asthma has provided Noni with companions: dead birds, moles, mice, beetles. Sometimes, sitting among the dead in a silence animated only by the breezes and the birds, a neighbor's voice, a curse, will sail directly overhead like a sharply beaked paper plane and Asthma will hear little Pea Pod receive a slap, followed by a howl, and then Goldie yelling, and the air around Faculty Circle will churn with trouble; trouble will grease the walls of Pea Pod's house. All the mothers are screamers. They cannot help themselves. But when she is happy, Goldie sits down at the piano, just as Noni used to do, except Goldie doesn't play Baconfelder or Bartók or Mussorgsky. She plays Irving Berlin and Cole Porter, Rodgers and Hammerstein. Once when Pea Pod refused to stop howling, Goldie played "There Is Nothin' Like a Dame" so loudly she declenched a thunderclap: the entire sky flew into a rage and it rained *buckets of black cats* (Blackie's words) for two whole days.

Asthma's own mother is *belleza* and when Goldie plays "Luck Be a Lady" and Blackie sings, she sings *con espirito.* But Asthma distrusts these performances and has come to absolutely loathe the piano. Because of this loathing, Asthma had managed to break Noni's heart. "You have the fingers," Noni had insisted. "You have the spirit and the talent. You have the *ear.*" But Asthma said if she ever played anything it would be the kettledrum. She could see herself tearing into that drum like nobody's business.

"Kettledrum!" Noni had gasped, throwing her hands into the air. "Kettledrum! And why not the triangle? Spoons? Tacky crystal glassware? Why not dig wells and operate an elevator!" (Asthma did not tell her that the best time she ever had at the movies was when Harpo Marx tore that piano apart.)

When Asthma gets home, Blackie is relaxing in the tub. Her hair is turbaned, her rosy flesh buoyant and bestilled. Blackie and her Rod are going to Goldie's for cocktails and Asthma is expected to play with Pea Pod, but play at what? Asthma and Pea Pod have had a painful history ever since the time Asthma bullied Pea Pod and was bitten on the arm. For this Pea Pod had received a searing punishment. Goldie had thrown her over a shoulder, torn off her panties, and ascended the staircase swatting Pea Pod ragefully before tossing her like a sack of cornmeal into her room—as Asthma and Blackie stood in the front hall transfixed.

The following morning a freak ice storm had split a majestic cherry tree in two—a tree that had been the pride of Faculty Circle, planted smack in its middle. Asthma shudders recalling this, recalling her own terrific guilt, her wish that Pea Pod had done her greater damage—broken her arm or ruptured a vein. She has feared Pea Pod ever since. She imagines her in her room alone, drinking black milk, eating black food, and picking at a scab. "I'm *not* playing with Pea Pod," she says decisively. "I'm tired and hungry and I'm going to eat a peanut-butter-marshmallow sandwich."

"Sure, baby . . . ," Blackie yawns and closes her eyes. Asthma sees her mother's pecan-colored pubic hair fizzing in the perfumed bath salts.

—

He is unlike other people. And the girl, too, unlike other people. Sometimes when he is crouching alone in the lilacs waiting for the moment to quicken, for the world to start over, it does. Suspended in the shadows, he sees her windows come to life and when this happens it is as if the first stars have caught fire and he is vividly alive, he embodies expectation, flush with longing for a look at the One Child, the One Girl: Asthma. Whose parents, Blackie and her Rod, have just left the house and in cocktail attire walk to Goldie's front door and ring. In a moment they vanish as into a black hole. They will drink and drink. Propelled into a very great distance, time will stand still.

Asthma carries her supper to her room and considers her holdings: 110 animals (he has counted them) made of plastic, glass, wood—and one ivory elephant. They are provided with a restaurant that serves blue-plate specials, an amusement park constructed of shoe boxes, a castle with a moat, a movie theater (Italian. Made of printed cardboard and a gift from Noni). A mirror pond. An opera house, the Eiffel Tower, the Tower of Pisa (made of plaster), a locomotive.

The first time he saw Asthma she was in a tree. He had already seen Blackie, a hot machine made of rivets and spinning gears, like a pressure cooker and a robot combined. She was much like his own mother, always heating up and letting off steam. Asthma was better off in the tree than in the house.

Asthma's father, a history professor, collects stamped postcards from Jamaica going back to the 1850s. His prizes include the King of Wings Penitentiary featuring a pink Cunard Line stamp, and the Jehovah God Bible School with three Jamaica Boy Scout stamps: pink, blue, and green.

Stub has never taken food from Asthma's house.

It is unclear if he crouches among the lilacs to watch over Asthma or simply to watch her. If he could, he would join in her play. It is possible that he wishes to *be* her, wading deep into the fullness of the game. Upstairs framed in light, Asthma leans over her realm, moving things around. She is Ptah, brooding over the Egg of the World; she is Trimurti, her arms wheeling from within the lotus flower; she is Marduk, constructing a reed mat on the face of the waters, scattering dust, inventing gods and men— except that she plays with little glass horses, a plastic camel. He thinks Vanderloon would also appreciate this play of hers.

He burns as he watches her from below, the flickering, the firefly child, now you see her, now you don't—careening like the smallest particle of matter, as restless as a thing can be, as a puppy, an angel dancing on a pin, as a dust mote swimming in the ocean of the eye: rabbit, fairy, human child: Asthma! Sprite, little daemon, his own talisman burning from his neck, burning within the iris of his eye.

It is hard to see her without entering into a certain . . . delirium. But he has always been vulnerable. He navigates his loneliness as if on a raft with a tattered sail.

His pockets rattle with wire scraps he uses to pick locks. In a storm he needs every muscle of his slender frame to hold his bucking world together. Sometimes the raft breaks beneath him and he comes close to a thing so terrifying that it has no name.

All around him people are living their lives. All those lives! Mammals barely evolved in houses with clean windows and solid oak doors. Their refrigerators stocked with boxed butter and beef, mustard and beer. Often the smell of baking wafts from a kitchen window. The lawns speak of tranquility and community. He knows the best kitchens. On a balmy evening he naps on a well-tended lawn listening to music from a phonograph, munching a fresh cookie, the music reedy and strange, or lovely, as it is tonight, something from a distant place and time beyond his knowledge or comprehension. The divine voices of the choir—angels or archons—tumbling through the air. The music nourishes him. It sweetens him with something like joy.

Once, the beautiful Dr. Ash, mathematician, stepped outside and stood on the grass alone in her bathrobe, fresh from a shower, her hair tumbling to her shoulders in grapes, and he kept still, on his back in the shadows, beneath a tree deep in leaf, so still she did not see that he was there. He heard her sigh and say aloud: *Why am I so sad?* It was a thing he had never thought to ask himself. He marveled at this. And ever after he would ask of himself: *Why am I so sad?*

It is impossible for him to imagine what it must be to live in a house as Dr. Ash does, full of quiet rooms, closets full of clothes, light summer linens and heavy woven wool; clothes for every season. Everything in the house warm and thick and heavy—as if each night it were basted in gravy. *These people,* he thinks, *live like the gods. Forever. Safe from the swift wheels of failure—and destitution.*

He watches the stars. He imagines renaming them. Offering them to Asthma freshly minted, freshly imagined. *The lost umbrella. The tin spoon. The little molecules. The peacock's tail. The cherry basket. The falling tears. The wandering souls. The sandman. The lost soul. The turtle's dilemma. The volcanic eruption. The kiss. Those who lament. The battling dogs. God's beard. The snail. The tree of life. The outer garment. The boiling pot. The fishhook and the leviathan. The burning rushes. The victim.* And those at the heart of the universe: a big black house on fire, the flames dancing in every window, smoke spilling from the cracks. *The stolen chicken!*

He had once stolen a freshly roasted chicken that had been left to cool on the kitchen counter. The family's Labrador retriever was scolded and made to spend the night in an ignominious little doghouse he had outgrown years before. No one noticed the missing kitchen towel Stub had used to carry the chicken off, which became his plate, tablecloth, and napkin.

The memory of that chicken makes him aware of just how hungry he is, and he considers breaking his one rule and checking out Blackie's larder. Asthma, after all, is busy at play, and Blackie and her Rod busy at drink. The little party is in full swing. He can hear Blackie telling Blondie about the book she is writing: *The Boy Beamed to Mars*. "*A Boy Beamed to Mars* is better," Goldie offers; it's more mysterious. Blackie puzzles this over. "I don't see what a damned difference it makes," she snaps, her blood pressure rising. "You have a tin ear," Goldie says. "That's why." "If I had a tin ear," Blackie hisses, "Brunelleschi would have told me. *The Boy Beamed to Mars* is exactly . . . it means he's *chosen*, goddamnit. He's *the* boy, not just *any* boy. Jesus." "*A* boy is more mysterious," Goldie insists, popping a maraschino cherry between her teeth. "He's already floating in space. He's anybody's boy, not chosen by some dickhead divinity . . . but why do I give a shit?"

"Yeah," Blackie agrees. "Why?" She stands, barely able to sustain herself. "WHY DON'T YOU JUST . . . JUST *NOT* GIVE A SHIT?" And she stomps off; the two men watch her leave without much interest.

When Blackie walks in the front door, Stub is standing at the foot of the stairs. "Who the hell?" she barks.

"I'm, uh, a student of Dr. Ash's," Stub mutters. "She told me to drop by and pick up some books. She said they'd be here, in the front hall, on a table, but—"

"Wrong house." Blackie says it vaguely as she weaves her way to the living room, shedding her heels as she goes. "Wrong house," she mutters and falls, not onto the sofa as she intends, but onto the floor. Stub runs to her, asks her what he can do.

"Go fuck yourself," says Blackie.

"The boy carries a burden of strangeness." Goldie's Rod says dreamily, prodding the ice in his glass with his tongue.

"Poor Timmy," Goldie agrees. She wonders how Timmy, the son of the Distempers across the street, can possibly grow into a man. And yet he is fifteen, almost a man— such a worrisome thought. "Poor Timmy," Goldie says again. "Fifteen and yet he moves along the ground like a crab."

"Like a crab with an ancient woe and an oversized barnacle stuck to his claw," her Rod agrees.

"When he walks about," Blackie's Rod wonders aloud, "I wonder where he goes?"

"Where does such a boy go to find a little comfort?" Goldie ponders.

"Sauerbraten," Goldie's Rod says decisively, his nose probing the air around him. "The boy won't starve."

"Genius," says Blackie's Rod, "needs to be squeezed. In that way it is like toothpaste. It needs . . . what was I getting at?" He sips his rye and frowns.

"I admit I don't quite follow," sighs Goldie. "Genius thrives on being cramped. Souls need, souls need . . . what do they need? Oh! I know! Souls need a *tight squeeze*!" She laughs merrily. "Perhaps Timmy is the one who will save us all."

"Someone said, someone . . . ," yawns Blackie's Rod, "that each and every one of us is meant to save the world. Timmy has been squeezed enough to become a cosmologist or one of those rare birds who invents bombs. You know, Little Boys!"

"And Fat Men!" trills Goldie. Faraway sobs can be heard. "That will be Timmy."

"A galaxy away," the Rods say together.

"Is it Pea Pod?" Goldie wonders.

"I believe it is Timothy," her Rod sighs. "Do we have nuts? I am desirous of nuts."

"In the pantry," Goldie directs him. "An entire can of cashews with its key. You'll have to get them yourself. I am unwilling, perhaps unable, to move."

"As am I," Goldie's Rod says, leaning back in his chair. "I'm in an immobilizing mood. Somewhere between contentment and anxiety."

"Remember when I said if we had a . . . a (what in the devil are they called?) a *child*, we were not to strike it?" Goldie startles her husband into chewing his ice.

"Better to strike them than paint them in honey and set them down hog-tied beside a hill of fire ants."

"Oh you bad boy," Goldie approves quietly into her glass, her tongue cold and pink. "In a little while I'll fry the three of us some eggs, I mean four, . . . but not just yet." she decides.

"Sunny-side down?" her Rod wonders. "With a spot of curry, love?"

"You can curry your own goddamned egg," says Goldie.

—

Teaching is not Blackie's Rod's greatest strength, yet this is what he does—although perhaps not for long, as his tenure is in question. His insufficiencies in that domain plague him. As he nurses his ice and rye he soothes his mind with thoughts of a domain that over the years has grown in holdings and complexities. Somewhere in Jamaica. This Jamaica of his is suspended somehow in a parenthetical time both before and after slavery. His own holdings include a big white colonial house studding a green hill, a lawn extending to the sea, plantations, serviceable natives.

Somewhere in Jamaica . . . those three words are all it takes to evoke a reverie that fits him like a diver's suit. He grows sugarcane. He makes molasses, sugar, rum. Perched in a town near the clouds, he can see this sugarcane spill like a broad river to the horizon. And his fields of plantain, banana, coconut, lime. He raises sheep for mutton and spring lamb. From where he sits, he can see these sheep munching. Out at sea, fishermen are returning, raising their voices in song. The sun is setting, the sky flushed pink; there will be roast lamb for supper, following the spiny-lobster bisque and, let's see . . . a pudding set on fire with his very own rum! From time to time he fetches a bottle from his cellar; already he can hear the starched white cotton of the black help crackling behind their knees. How pretty they are, Jamaican women, the color of gingerbread, of dark chocolate, milk chocolate, café au lait, toast, as they move about in the cool shadows of the downstairs rooms, setting out candles, flowers, a freshly pressed linen tablecloth, a Venetian carafe (the only thing he actually owns, inherited from a rich aunt on his mother's side). He allows himself the leisure to think about what it would be like to tumble into bed with all of them. He thinks it would be like taking a dip in chocolate mousse rich with eggs and cream. How many are there? He has, over the years, named them all after gems: Jade, Ruby, Pearl, Sapphire, Opal . . . and the new one, Heart of Mary, ugly, straight from Jehovah God Bible School— she keeps things running smoothly and sometimes rides his knees. Her little churchy clitoris as hot as a toasted raisin on his bare knee. Shameless, droll little Mary, so full of tricks. Speaking of which—has Pea Pod, sent to a corner, had her supper? His dear little Pea Pod. "Goldie!" He calls out as if she was elsewhere, picking orchids at the lawn's far end, "Goldie?"

"I'm here," she breathes. "Are we all ready for eggs? Shall I make a move to move? Or . . . maybe in a little while . . ."

Out at sea a large ship approaches. He's sold his rum for beef, wheat flour; a French baker is onboard, too! A fat Flemish blond. Or Swiss, to milk the cows. To be worth its salt a mousse needs a dollop of whipped cream. Sacks of Italian polenta, Indonesian rice, and bottled mincemeat (where the devil is mincemeat bottled? Wales?).

Oysters. He sends Ruby, her petticoats flashing, down the path to the beach to greet the oystercatchers, the boys who bring in mussels, too. Clams! Abalone. Sweet abalone!

"Sweet abalone . . . ," he says aloud, almost singing.

"Who's that?" Goldie wonders. "Rod? Are you seeing someone?"

And scallops. The sea appears to boil there are so many scallops. Lobster! And eel . . . , "Sapphire!" he calls out. "Fish stew!"

"Fiddies don't stew," says Goldie. "They fwim."

How wonderful it is in Jamaica. Far in the distance, far out to sea, he hears Blackie's Rod say dreamily:

"Say, Goldie. How're you set for bacon?"

"Bacon?" says Goldie. "Wha's that?"

●

"Who are you?" Pea Pod asks Stub. She's wandering around with a can of cashews, its top peeled back and sharp as a razor. "Why are you sitting on my daddy's grass?"

"I'm from abroad," Stub tells her. "In my country there's no private property. I apologize. Say! Look at this . . ." He pulls a toy gyroscope from his pocket.

"What does it do?" Pea Pod eyeballs the thing, intrigued.

"Let me show you."

—

Later, stretched out on the sumptuous Boethius sleeping bag he stole from the Sandor Methinks dorms—the classiest on campus—he ponders the nature of his difficulty. What *was* his difficulty, exactly? Why was it that as far back as he could recall, he had never inhabited his own skin, had always been an outsider to everyone, even himself? Trees he could speak to, relate to—and in this way he was very like a child. Yet this, he thinks, must be, *is* a good thing because children are good. Even little Pea Pod with her temper and pinched face is *good*! Yes, he is certain of this, recollecting his own brief moment in the garden when he *did* fit in his own skin and was good, was happy. If one could—despite all that transpires to undo the infant's marvelous capacity for joy—continue to live, at one's core, the life of the child, well then one would never cease to radiate out in all directions! As if . . . as if . . . as if one's own navel were a sun! A blazing star, forever burning!

Things. He has few. The Boethius sleeping bag, a Swiss Army knife, a duffel (another Boethius, olive green, studded with real brass) that holds his limited, if acceptable, wardrobe. He has toothbrushes, toothpaste, secreted under sinks all over the place—the library, gym, kitchens, Utilities House, cabin in the woods—and there's a small box of his stuff (galoshes, talcum powder) under the Provost's porch.

The things belonging to others he considers as objects featured in a vanitas, made of clay, plastic, wood, glass, metal, and so forth; sometimes he comes upon a small thing of jade or cinnabar or lacquer, and in the penumbra of evening, the dawn light of early fall, the sweaty heat of August, takes it up gently and turns it this way and that as if looking at something from another world. He looks at other people's dining room tables, their bed boards and fire tongs. Once, he stood outside a window gazing at Dr. Ash's glass of port forgotten on a coffee table, radiating light. Sometimes he gets lost in the spine of a book, a bottle of milk, a scarf of yellow silk.

Yet he is not the only madman about! After all, there is Professor Brunelleschi, mad with pain, speaking to his wife sometimes for over an hour in the evening: *Amore. My eye. The eye of my heart, my beloved, my violet button, my tangible rainbow, my exuberance, my youth, my tongue! Noni! I have forgotten how to laugh. I drink tears in the evening's soup! I piss tears! Without you I become stranger by the day. I swim in my pants* . . . And in all the houses, the little radios, now pierced with windows the colors of looming bad weather, percolating with a senator named Ratmutterer: *Rabble-rousers! Brooding eggheads! They cook their pernicious rumors in pink, pink casseroles made by Soviets reeking of unwashed—*

Stub covers his ears. Runs to the library. *It's a good place, the library. One is left to oneself. It is like you are a tree or a receptacle for cans. Once a professor asked me my major. I was reading beneath the bull's-eye window in Sciences. Science, I said. He asked why. I thought about it. Then I said: I enjoy knowing why things move. Nothing ever stands still. Things are always rising and falling, growing and shrinking. I began to feel an old fear rising and couldn't go on. He said: I know exactly what you mean. It's exhausting. And he wandered off chuckling.*

But today. Someone—a Professor Emeritus, I think he said he was—named William Sweetbriar, "Billy," introduced himself. And when he asked I told him my best lie: I was on a Fulbright from New South Wales, Australia. And I was working on the Vanderloon papers. I got carried away. I hadn't actually talked to anybody for over six months and suddenly I was a chatterbox!

"All the way from New South Wales to study Loon!" he cried out. "I know Loon, of course. Knew him. As well as he allowed. We were colleagues, of course. And his library! Of course you have access to the library!"

"Well, it's in boxes, sir. Not yet inventoried . . . ," I said, the merest hint of an Australian accent now coloring my speech. And then he asked me the question I feared.

"You're working with Harvey? Old Pemble?" He snickered and winked, sharing an obscure joke.

"No." I smiled as best I could. "The, the new . . . he's visiting, from . . . Oxford: Welch. He's here briefly, I gather. Filling in for . . ."

"Pemble! Of course! I'd forgotten he's abroad. I'm out of touch." Billy sighed. "With the department I mean. You hit a certain age you're so busy oiling your joints and calming your rashes, your stomach gasses—you've no time for much else. What's your name, son?" And I said, and I have no idea why I said this, but I said:

"My name is Charter Chase."

"Entre nous, Charter," Billy whispered fiercely, "You're lucky Old Pemble is abroad. Well, I'm off! But . . ." He looked deeply into my eyes as if reading me and said: "But I should make you dinner, lonely scholar that I suppose you are."

●

A can is kicked, he sees it rise above the dust and for an instant catch fire in the light of the moon. Asthma is "it." She stands with her foot on the can in triumph as the others return to the Circle. She closes her marvelous eyes and begins to count. If Vanderloon could see her, he would say that Asthma is currently the "superior principle." She plays the part of the bird; the others play the fish. And the bird always catches the fish. It is never the other way around.

Somewhere hidden among the darkest of cosmic star houses, Pea Pod weeps. Her tears are just another thread in the fabric of time. Time—that obstinate, irascible persona non grata, a finger in every pie. He looks at the can. There it is, casting a shadow, like a dolmen for an ant. Right at the center of everything.

A shout! Asthma is triumphant! Having caught her first fish, crouching behind the Tutweiler's orgone box.

Somewhere in the sky the sobbing has silenced, at least for now. The sound of the evening news rises to the stars and like a venomous ink of squids hooked to a rusting respirator, canned laughter oxidizes in the air. Gratified by the vision of Asthma owning the can with her foot, that triumphant stance, the way she tilts her head to one side, her hand over her eyes as she counts, her short brown hair stirring in the breeze, he decides to call it a day and returns to his current refuge, the spotless Utilities House, where a nice jar of elderberry jam, made by the Provost's visiting sister-in-law, and a new loaf of Wonder Bread await him.

The next day everything changes . . .

—

Everything changes. Because Billy, Professor Emeritus, lonely, long in tooth, all angles, all elbows and knees (and he has always been this way, graceful and unwieldy at the same time, his broad shoulders holding it all together), open-faced, of sunny disposition, an optimist, wearing a cotton shirt the color of Dijon mustard, hunts down Charter Chase and finds him.

"There you are!" he says. "I've been looking all over. Been prowling the stacks!" He puts out his hand and they shake, like gentlemen. Billy cuts to the chase. "Charter," he says, "I've been wondering about . . . well. About your *digs*. Are they adequate?"

"Ah . . . well . . ." Charter laughs uncomfortably. "You know what it is like to be a poor student, but—"

"Of course I do!" Billy cries. "Indeed I do! So here's the thing, son," and he pats Charter on the shoulder paternally (or so Charter supposes, having never received anything like this from his father). "I live alone, " Billy continues as they make their way together down the steep library steps and into the full light of day. "The house is far too big. I barely enter the upstairs. There's an entire living space up there, bedroom, bath, study." They approach Faculty Circle and he points to one of the several gracious faux-Tudor houses with pitched roofs and screened-in porches. The stucco façade is a pleasant shade of sand, the wooden window frames painted a rich chocolate. "The place is ship-shape of course. Nicely kept up by buildings and grounds. But I imagine you are familiar with the Circle."

Charter is not only familiar with the Circle, but with Billy's house. It was Billy's countertop that had once provided him with a cooling pie. Charter nods. Says, "Yes. The Provost had a little get-together for the foreign students a while ago—"

"Of course!" Billy considers his rehearsed delivery. "Uh," he says. "Here's the thing. Here you are, a Fulbright scholar far from home living—or so I imagine—in inadequate housing and, well, surely you can see where I am coming from."

"Sir. I do. I do. I do not dare . . . it's too kind, far too kind." Charter runs his fingers through hair he knows is in need of some attention, and which Billy addresses at once.

"Have you, have you . . . been to an American barber?"

"No, sir—"

"Billy."

"No, Billy. Short on funds and as you can see I am personally not too handy in that direction."

"I'll take you to town. I know a good man there. Now, the upstairs is nicely done up." They stand together on the Circle now, looking at his house, which shares a lawn and a lilac hedge with Asthma's.

"Terrific closets. Full use of the screen porch," Billy says, "the kitchen. Do you cook?"

"No—"

"Of course not. You are busy. With Loon! Who could have imagined this! My own days of being busy are over. I'll cook for the two of us. I am bored cooking for myself. Losing touch! Look at this scar." He throws a hand into Charter's face. "Trimming a radish." He thrusts the tip of a thumb into his mouth and sucks it. "I am, therefore, in all simplicity, no strings attached, proposing a proper dwelling, nicely done up by Margaret, who blessedly is gone to Wisconsin and out of our hair, yours and mine. One of the perks of being a college professor—in case of divorce, the professor cannot give the spouse the house! My campus digs are . . . *on* the house! *On* the house!" He laughs almost to tears, raving as they pace together around the Circle. I'll get the upstairs tidied up and then, Charter, it's yours. In the meantime, come for supper. Are you free?" Charter nods. "Six. I'll show you your digs, get the cleaning lady—she'll be here later in the week—to give the place a thorough . . . Do you need help moving?"

"Sir, Billy. You will be amazed by the little I have. My things, such a nuisance, but it's o.k., really, were *lost in transit*. The authorities . . . *nothing doing!*" (Already Charter was picking up on Billy's manner of speech.) "Nothing doing! But, hey! I get by! On a shoestring, of course . . ."

"That's my boy!" Billy slaps Charter on the back. "Till six!" And off he goes.

Charter has a new good-looking back pack purloined from Hum Hall at the final semester's end a month earlier: solid canvas duck, color of good tobacco, hand sewn, leather trim and straps—a Brunchhauser! He will pick up a pair of serviceable rubber-soled leather boots, heavy for the season but good for walking the woods, a top-of-the-line sweater, and two handsome striped shirts, all currently in a gym locker. He makes his way to the gym and showers, thinking: *This could be good. Despite the risks. The heavy price if discovered.* Then, suddenly ecstatic, he roars. That night he writes:

The chapel bells guide my hours. To their chimes (every fifteen minutes!) time unspools, the seasons and their constellations

*spill across campus like a sea. I set off for Billy's a few minutes
before six and arrived just as the bells chimed:*

   Doing! Dang! Doing!

   Doing! Dang! Doing!

*As I walked up the Old Boy's path holding my head high, I
considered the nature of destiny. A garden snake rode the grass
beside me, the smell of garlic and tomatoes stimulated every
nerve in my body, and a flock of swifts disturbed the quiet blue
of the sky:* And let fowl fly above the earth in front of the
vault of Heaven. *(Vanderloon quoting the Bible.)*

—

Billy could not be happier having *popped the question* (a
silly way to put it!). Once, he had popped the question to
Margaret (fatal mistake!); this time he has simply offered
a few vacant rooms to a young scholar. But loneliness has
been leeching the marrow from his bones and as he tends
to supper, rinsing greens thoughtfully, stirring spaghetti
sauce, exuberance overtakes him. The boy, he is certain,
will be an easy, grateful companion. He needs attending
to; there's something unfinished about him; he's wounded
somehow, much too thin, older than his years. Billy will
feed him the meals he does best: spaghetti, beef with
gravy—solid American middle-class fare—along with some
of the great dishes of Normandy he came to love during
summers spent abroad. Billy also bakes a pie. (Once, he
had baked a perfect rhubarb pie that had volatilized as it

cooled on the counter. He liked to say it was a miracle: *That pie was so flawless it went to Heaven!* But things did have a way of going missing on the Circle. Goldie insisted it was poltergeists.)

Billy sets the table. He grates the Parmesan, sets out a small bowl of red-pepper flakes, and sprinkles a pinch of oregano into the sauce for its final fifteen minutes. Precisely at six Charter arrives and the two sit down to supper, the one facing the other. Looking into a deep white dish brimming with hot noodles and large meatballs sweating juice, Charter is moved nearly to tears.

"Biblical!" he exclaims.

"Why biblical?" Billy wonders.

"It's ambrosial and . . . gives off beams of light!"

"You've been reading too much Loon," Billy jokes. "I've only served you a dish of spaghetti." Yet he is pleased. "Curious you say that, though . . ." He tells his young guest about the vanishing pie. Charter blushes, but briefly. Billy's innocence in the matter is evident. "Are you religious?"

"No," Charter tells him. "Although I like to consider just how horny Noah's toenails were when he hit six hundred."

"Moses had horns . . . ," Billy muses and then confides: "I am a private sort. Reclusive you could say. In this way I am much like your friend Vanderloon, although he has taken it to extremes. Perhaps campus life breeds recluses. Well. What I mean to say is you will find it quiet in the house. You will be able to work undisturbed. The Circle could not be more conducive to study. Well . . .

there are the children and they have their games, but still . . . they really don't create much disturbance. Let me show you your room!"

What impresses Charter about the house first of all is that there are no photographs, no family pictures on the mantel or sideboard, no dead parents, ancestors, pets. Apparently Billy is not only wifeless, he's childless. This is comforting. If there had been photos everywhere Charter would have felt like an intruder. But he thinks instead that he can do well here. He will enter into a serious study of Vanderloon's ideas, not just collect them as one collects curiosities. Not just wander in the books aimlessly.

The house is spare; apparently Margaret had brought along a great deal of family furniture that left the house when she did. Billy has gone for a certain modernist minimalism, uncommon on the Circle. The few pieces he has acquired are angular, blond, the lamps as disquieting as space aliens. On the walls are a few framed museum posters, someone named Rothko who Charter thinks must have been a house painter, and a Dalí that causes him so much anxiety he will stay clear of it during his tenure in the house. An inscrutable Boz Heiffer.

Together they climb the stairs and reach a hallway lit by a clearstory: the light! Billy leads him to a large room furnished with a desk and chair, a reading chair, and a number of those peculiar lamps, each one pointing at them accusingly. "Ah!" Billy laughs. "The cleaning lady, I don't know why . . ." He redirects them into a more serviceable angle.

Above the desk is a large window. Stub's heart leaps; his ears are ringing; he feels like singing: the room has an unobstructed view of Asthma's own.

▬

"What do you think?" Billy asks as they return to the living room and settle into the butterfly chairs. The chairs are a novelty and Charter thrills with a sudden surge of sophistication and expectation. As he sits, he acquires substance, he expands. The blond coffee table is wonderfully indefinable, almost . . . *numinous.* He thinks the word *numinous* ridiculous, thinks it ridiculous, too, that ever since he renamed himself so hastily and with such affectation, he is unrecognizable, risks turning into a fop.

"Do you like it? The upstairs; is it—"

"What is there not to like? Your unerring taste, your bountiful generosity, I—"

Billy reaches into a pocket and tosses him a key. "Not that you need it; I keep the place unlocked, we all do. The only thefts around here—and they are sporadic—appear to affect our pantries alone. The passing hobo, a mischievous undergraduate. Look here. Let's say you move in Friday night. We'll have dinner and then, well! The upstairs is yours. I trust you will work well there, that you will honor me and the house with a brilliant dissertation. Nothing, Charter, would please me more."

Outside, another game of kick the can begins. Asthma shouts: "No! Dickie! That's not *fair*! That's not the way we *do it*!" For a brief moment a medley of children's voices sweeps past. "That," Billy grins," is about as bad as it gets."

Later he stands outside the library, still as a stone. The evening grows darker and he stands beneath the great mystery of the night, the Circle house lights above him shining through a tapestry of leaves, making everything look extremely strange and beautiful. He imagines he is deep beneath the sea, a merman maybe, and that the lights are not house lights at all but stars glimmering through sea grass and water.

—

Blackie keeps breaking her nose. Twice in less than a year. She sits alone nursing her rye as her Rod is intangible up in his study, working on his book (publish or perish!), or so she supposes. Instead, from a distant hill deep within his mind, he is gazing at his magnificent house in Jamaica, burning white in the blazing sun, the rooms freshly scrubbed, tiles cool to the touch. (How he loves tile!)

Blackie gingerly touches her bandaged nose. She has enough self-knowledge to know the drinking, these periodic accidents, have much to do with guilt. The nasty way she treats Asthma, and this despite herself. She wishes she were nicer, knew how to control her irritation, keep her filthy mouth shut, or, better yet, manage a pleasant, an amusing (!), conversation. The truth is, she's always been nasty, she's never liked children; her annoyance, her impatience, is visceral. She has always been rude. She likes to think it doesn't mean anything but is up nights because she knows it does. She's a bitch at best, a shrew and a crab; she's shrill and she's into control. She pontificates like a nun or a nanny. Despite all the evidence to the contrary, she's convinced much of the time that she has a handle on the stuff that eludes everybody else.

Once, she caught Asthma rolling her eyes. "Don't you dare do that!" she had shrieked, "You nobody's fat bottom!" The recollection of scenes such as this torments her. *But I didn't slap her,* she thinks, tapping the bandaged tip of her nose. *It's not like I'm Goldie. I* know *what I'm doing. I struggle. It's* existential.

Looking across the Circle she sees that Billy is entertaining. His young guest is reading on the front porch. It's pleasant to see that porch in use again. It makes the Circle feel . . . companionable. It makes her feel less alone. As does the rye and the thought that her dilemma is somehow . . . heroic. She will do better. She will think of diversions. She will take Asthma places. Across the river to Kahontsi. Its museums. The theater. Buy Asthma a pinafore. Barrettes. She'll pack a picnic lunch. She'll get it right. *Nobody's fat bottom!* Where the hell did that come from? *Poor little worm,* she thinks, her heart sinking. *Poor little plucked hen.*

Billy has served his guest coffee and they sit together in conversation. The children are merry, running hither and yon; the evening is balmy, the stars turning on one by one, and the frogs! Their voices trilling from the nearby pond. *The world is a civilized place,* Blackie reminds herself. *If only I could remember.*

—

Early Friday evening. His duffel, so large he thinks he could have lived in it all along, is now emptied and stored on a shelf in the closet. He has hung his three shirts on sturdy wood hangers, folded his one good sweater with care and placed it in the middle dresser drawer, rolled up his three pairs of socks, his few pieces of underwear, and placed these in an upper drawer. His few toiletries are in the cabinet above the sink.

He has time for a nap before dinner but his heart is pounding. He is famished and the air smells of *fricassee* (Billy's word) . . . the mattress, chosen by Margaret, is impossibly luxurious, however, the bedspread the color of moonlight *(starched!)*, the sheets nacreous. He thinks he will sleep like a chosen child, suspended in a pearly haze. He is soothed by the thought that he is destined for far more than he ever supposed. He is about to become a legitimate entity with an entire suite at his disposal, right smack in the heart of Faculty Circle (but he must be cautious, discreet, patient). He gets not only to see her, devour her, drink her in—but (and why not?) to *talk* to her. Because he is a scholar of promise and charm come all the way from New South Wales to study one of theirs, the elusive genius Verner Vanderloon. When Billy calls up to him for supper, he is awakened from a surprisingly profound slumber. Hastily Charter pulls himself together and descends to find a table regally set (candles!); he is served farmed chicken, Billy's own rhubarb wine, biscuits. The carrots (how is this possible!) have been caramelized.

From the dining room window he can see that the brats are out in full number and a new game has begun . . . but Billy is speaking, and for how long?

". . . always at cross-purposes. But then, isn't that the nature of things, one moment undoing the next, the web spun only to be ripped to bits. Time compresses, time expands, and sometimes—as when one is in bed with the right person . . . ," he closes his eyes and nods in the direction of a distant memory, "ceases altogether. How many times have I stumbled? How many times have I gathered myself together and set off again? How many times triumphant— yes, *I have had my triumphs!*—only to fall on my face?" Billy's eyes fog with tears. "To tell the truth—"

The windows are open to the early summer evening. The brats' voices, the voices of frogs and crickets, locusts— surge and recede.

"Forgive me," Billy says. "I ramble on, I have become something of a fool. But I trust this, too, shall pass . . ."

"No fool, sir! Billy—"

"It will pass. My mood I mean. Not my foolishness!" The brats are playing hide-and-seek. Charter sees them scatter. They will hide behind the familiar houses, in window wells, down the backyard basement stairs, in the limbs of trees.

"All that honey spilled," Billy continues. (Or is it money spilled?) "All those fires stoked that might have been better left cold in their dead ashes; all the ice broken between the teeth; all the false starts, dreary roads taken—as meanwhile the stars pulsed blindly above!"

"You are a poet—"

"No, no, no . . ." Billy shakes his head, yet for an instant a wistful smile enlivens his face and Charter sees the boy he once was, the youth. "What's worse," Billy sighs, growing darker, "is that the signs were *there*. I mean: one should have attended to those pulsing stars and all the rest. Recalled the beauties one had ceased to see. The myriad beauties, Charter. Of the world, the mind, the flesh. The spirit, my boy." He clenches his teeth and sucks in the air. "The red flags. One must heed them!"

"Red flags?"

"Fog horns! Sirens! Rings around the moon! Oh! Fatality! Nevermore!" Billy ravens. "NEVERMORE!"

"Sir?"

"My marriage, for instance. To a woman who wielded a scythe."

"*That* deadly!"

"Too often," Billy ignores him, "I have *not paid attention.* Spilled the milk. Soiled the linens. And yet . . . and yet . . ."

Suddenly Asthma dashes past as wild as a fox and un-imaginably rich in life. And then she is gone, and Charter is irresistibly drawn to find her.

". . . and yet, Charter! How eagerly I longed for life. And still . . . longing . . . the *longing*! Even now!"

"You," Charter must force himself to speak, "have years ahead, *years*!"

"Bah!" Billy rises and goes to the kitchen where, aston-ishingly, he sticks his head under the cold-water faucet and gives himself a proper dousing before shaking his head vigorously from left to right like a wet dog. Charter rises to the occasion and hands him a clean dish towel.

"Good," Billy says and pats him on the shoulder. "Well done. Time to retire!" he decides. "Don't worry about the dishes . . . in the morning . . . I'll . . ." He wanders off.

Charter takes up the dishes and fills the sink with suds. His agitation has quieted. He can hear Blackie calling for Asthma, the other mothers calling (and one blows a whistle). Soon she will be in her room, tucked away for the night, a breath away from him. Lovingly he washes every-thing, gazing again and again at the Circle, the rich grass wet with color, the trim houses, their slate roofs and stone chimneys, the polished window glass. It all gleams. It is all wonderful.

Once everything has been dried and returned to its place, he steps out into the evening to smoke a Camel—a new habit he can currently "afford," having, on a visit to the train station down by the river, a pleasant hour's walk away, purloined the wallet of a well-heeled and permed crone on her way to the city for a hit of high culture. She had fallen into a deep nap beside the alligator purse, its mouth as open as its owner's. Charter thinks how over time such acts repeat themselves, each alike, each distinct: the local hunter, dashing in sideburns and well-oiled boots, his back pocket unbuttoned; a young coed devoid of common sense, her little silk purse abandoned on the ticket counter as she, tucked into the phone booth, catches up on gossip ($150 in bills!).

How good it is to smoke a cigarette, one's back against a solid wall, the breeze playing in the leaves, the Circle silenced, each window the promise of a shadow-puppet play. Pathos and terror, black comedy, tenderness and loss, fire and ice, pleasure and punishment—all this surging and ebbing in those ruthless, wondrous, persistent rooms. Such sweetness! Such menace! He looks on as lives grow stale, are renewed. As kittens grow into cats; as betrayal rustles the sheets, rolls under the crib, and comes to rest there; as Death catches a glimpse of a maiden and cannot turn away.

I am a part of this, he thinks, taking it all in. *A shadow among the many. Not sleeping in the library among boxes or in reeking cabinets or in the woods but in a bed big enough to sail the seas on, squeaky with soap, dined and wined (my ear bent out of shape but everything has its price).*

Just before Jenny had been sent away she had told Stub: "We soon will all be mad, as mad as a person can be, as mad as you and I." And Stub had said:

"I'm not mad! Little kids aren't ever mad!"

"The maddest," she had told him gently. "The maddest of all."

Now that Asthma, Pea Pod, and all the brats have vanished into their houses for the night, Charter ponders what she meant. He thinks she meant this: a child knows nothing else, nothing but the madness that preys upon it relentlessly, the madness that is in the food it eats, the words it hears, the dreams that, having failed to protect it, turn upon it. He thinks that from afar Jenny has directed him to the very place he now stands. It is his task to be vigilant. To assure that Asthma will come through childhood unscathed. He makes a promise to Asthma and to himself. He makes a promise to Jenny.

—

Asthma's room glows with light. Dressed in flannel pajamas illuminated with starfish, sea horses, porpoises, and fresh from her evening bath, she hovers above a ping-pong table forested with plastic pine trees and all the rest. Squinting, he can just make out her little earnest face orbiting the table; round and round she goes. He has seen the mirror pond up close, the Italian opera house; he has held an ivory elephant to his cheek, counted geese and sheep—and here's the thing: It is she who gives a shape to the shapeless, the formless days, the lost, the fragmented days. Her face. The games she plays. Her voice calling out across the lawn. The noise the can makes when she gives it a kick; her scolding tones when Dickie or another of the brats aggravates her . . . all this makes it possible for him to breathe quietly, to get *on with it*—his life, such as it is. Her tiny frame, her wrists (like a bird's), her sprawling tabletop town, her faded frocks, her mop of short hair, her gleeful laughter, her little buckled shoes . . .

Because before Asthma, his days were hollowed out as if by a spoon and he would enter them as a blind man enters an unknown hotel, tap-tapping across the threshold into the formless minutes and hours—and this before the night would steal up on him, the night with its own relentless demands. Cloaked in black feathers, his mouth full of clay, he would practice survival in the face of the incommensurable. But now!

He sees her moving in her own special way with her own special grace. And oh! The miracle! Asthma looks out—she always does this before going to sleep—for a glimpse of Peter Pan, an owl, a Martian, maybe a witch. And she tells them all: *Protect me or let me be.* Godless herself, this is the way Asthma prays each night: *Protect me or let me be.* Her mantra is now his own. *Let me be as well,* he says to the darkness. *Let us both be.* Tonight the things that bite and squall and snap and bark, fly from his mind and Charter is possessed by the best of the night. That is to say he sleeps.

But despite this sweet enchantment, he awakens in the dark hole of early morning—three o'clock, when once wolves were about, wild dogs. Often he awakens like this, his heart overleaping, and there is nothing to do but attend to the hour's imperatives, abandon the bed, and move about. He enters the office, its eye on Asthma's window, now darker than the sky, and it seems as he looks out that his heart, still pounding, is made of a muscled cable that reaches to that window and latches on, as a lamprey's mouth latches on to the body of a fish. And he sits, immobile, as Asthma sleeps, the two of them stuck to the skin of the world as it spins. In this way Charter is no longer solitary but part of the fabric of things. He appreciates the night and its wandering points of light, its lawns turned the color of blackberry jelly, its gravel smoothed to tweed, its owls tearing at the throats of mice. He is bountiful with love.

But . . . what is this? Someone is out and about wandering the Circle all alone. Barely visible, her form is distinctive, and her movements recognizable. It is the beautiful, bewildered Dr. Ash, barefoot and wearing a silk kimono. She sits down beneath the tree that marks the Circle's navel and rolls her forehead from knee to knee, back and forth, back and forth, her hair billowing from her scalp like smoke. He watches as she folds herself into a ball and remains there like that for a very long time.

This is what I have learned during the early morning vigils. Depending on one's state of mind, the hours pass painfully slowly, like a cold clay moving beneath the placid surface of a river—or they collapse all of a sudden and there is the sun (!)

rising in the east and one's own head awkwardly resting on the top of an unfamiliar desk and the day has come and Dr. Ash is not to be seen and Billy is already under sail and I can smell the coffee . . .

—

Domestic life is his, unexpected and unprecedented. After an early breakfast, a new day unfolds. The brats have vanished and so he attends to the work at hand, the confection of a spurious dissertation, a marvelous creature of the mind, neither here nor there: a chimera, half fur, half feather. A thing feasible and resembling nothing else; a midnight blossom; an entire world in levitation; a thing both beaked and lipped . . .

He is looking at *Ancient Roots and Ways*, at Vanderloon's eccentric sketches of Quetzalcoatl sitting on top of a volcano. He appears to be wearing a garment made of leopard skin. He is looking at the sun-god of Babylon rising from the world-mountain, lightning leaping from the flesh of his outstretched arms. Quetzalcoatl is wearing an extravagant pronged hat and appears to be holding the toothed jawbone of a crocodile. Charter dreams over the zodiac belonging to the ancient Hebrews, in which Cancer finds its roots in a flood so powerful it causes the world to spin backwards—just as a crab moves backwards.

And this evasive movement of the crab appeals to him immensely. It opens a way. And Charter sees just what it is he will write about. The solution to his dilemma burns into his consciousness the way a meteor burns into the earth's atmosphere, blazing a trail. He will invent a people unknown to all but Vanderloon. A decision that is monumental, exciting, and irrational. There is no reason why he should do this. But he has spent his life in hiding, fearful of discovery. Perhaps he fears honest scholarship can only fail, appear vastly flawed to those he will likely one day encounter. He fears it is inevitable that sooner or later he will have to justify himself. He wishes he had paid more attention to Axel's admonitions. Axel who was clearly distressed Stub had not yet read *Coming of Age in Samoa*. Axel who had once suggested that Stub enter the study of Verner Vanderloon as others enter a religious order.

Yet in a moment Charter is off and running. He will invent the papers, notes, some rare editions unavailable but for Vanderloon's own personal library, stowed away and moldering in boxes abandoned by the very institution he had devoted his life to, revealing or having revealed the mysteries of the human imagination with how many generations of eager minds.

Vision is one thing, Vanderloon had liked to say, *and observation is another.* When on Easter Island he had learned of the bird's superiority over the fish, he understood in a flash what informed that entire culture. He *saw* that the Easter Islanders were themselves like raptors, snapping away at one another until there was nothing left. *Easter Island,* Vanderloon wrote in *Rules of Rage, is the mirror of all that is wrong with a species that again and again snaps up the fish rather than attempt to understand it.* Today Charter puzzles over this. He thinks he does not want to be either one. He wants to survive but not snap anybody up in the process. A *hare* is what he wants to be. The one that with a leap, disappears.

That evening when Billy hands him a slice of quiche, Charter is ready to speak about his dissertation.

"It is an unusual project," he begins. He gazes at the quiche, gemmy with scallions, peppers, cubes of ham. "Perhaps you will find it odd . . ."

"No! No! Surely not!"

"Well, for one thing, Vanderloon is obscure. Unacknowledged. You must know that when he retired he was given one small pewter bowl—"

"No! How dreadful! The OED is customary, or some rare volume. For the women perhaps a sterling-silver charger—"

"Charger?"

"A . . . shallow dish. A *big* one. But a small *pewter* bowl! How terrible! How is this possible?"

"Five people showed up at the dinner. The table was set for thirty."

"No!"

"Yes. Yes! So . . . there is *that.*"

"I'm speechless. It is true I didn't even go myself!"

"And, well, the material that interests me is obscure. I am reading unpublished and scattered notes. I am reading little-known publications, small editions, many bound in paper. It may be that much of this exists only in those boxes in the library. Some printed on paper of such poor quality it crumbles at the touch."

"Fabulous! Charter! This is exciting!"

"But wait! It gets worse!"

"Worse!" Billy clasps his hands. "Worse! Wonderful! Please go on!"

"Much of my personal interest has to do with a small island, so small as to be ignored on most maps. And, well, I have been there—"

"You have! Are you saying you and Loon? No one else?"

"No one else. Which is why—"

"Yes! Yes! I understand! One might say the two of you belong to a very select club!"

"It goes deeper. Vanderloon is like a father." At this Billy finds himself resentful of Vanderloon, jealous perhaps. "I owe him everything," Charter continues. "Three years ago I read an article of his published in the *New South Wales Observer.* About the island. I decided at once to go. It was not easy to get there. I sailed alone."

"My god!"

"The island is . . . untouched. Vanderloon, exemplary in his reticence, his rigor, his humility—"

"I had no idea!"

"—made friends there. They revealed—"

"Secrets!"

"Yes. All that is—in his words—*unbeholdable*—"

"Loon beheld!"

"The secret of an ancient, a virgin tradition."

"*Virgin*, you say!"

"Untouched. Unbroken. Pristine."

—

Any number of birds are performing on the branches. But for their bellies—these birds have white bellies just like some fish—they are a dirty brown. Dr. Ash thinks they look sorrowful. Sorrowful birds the colors of fish belly and dung. She thinks that if they wore vests they would be secondhand and knitted of cheap yarn.

It is ten o'clock in the morning and already the day is over. Beautiful Dr. Ash, her raven hair falling to her shoulders in clumps a recent lover had seized in his fists, is talking to a jade plant. *All* her love affairs end in disaster; they begin with a shimmer but before you know it everyone is sobbing and shuddering.

The wonderful things about Dr. Ash are her hair and her breasts, which are set high and far apart. Also her mind. She has a magnificent mind if you appreciate mathematics. (There are twelve people in the world who understand her when she speaks about what she knows best and loves the most.)

Recently she heard on the radio that plants communicate with people. She immediately drove to the florist in Ohneka and bought a jade plant. She thinks that living with a jade plant is like living with an obstinate introvert.

●

Charter sets off for the library, head high, freshly sudsed, caffeinated, having polished off a preposterous breakfast (his host *warms* the maple syrup and serves the French toast with a dollop of whipped cream). He cannot help himself but must take the Circle the long way so as to pass Asthma's house. There at the edge of the lawn, just behind the low hedge, he finds her crouching beside a fallen log swarming with large black beetles as shiny as polished buttons, their one red queen moving dramatically among them. Asthma looks up and sees him.

"Who are you, anyway?" she asks.

"The . . . uh . . . Fulbright student," he manages. "From next door."

"That means you're bright, then." She says it solemnly. "And full of—"

"Don't say I'm full of myself. I'm not. I'm full of French toast."

"Why are you always poking around?"

"Am I?"

"What do they call you?"

"My name? You must mean my name?" She nods. Her eyes poke into his like two sharp twigs. "Charter."

"Look at the beetles," she demands. "Why is one so red?" He steps over the hedge and crouches beside her.

"She is their Papesse."

"Papesse!" Asthma screams with laughter. "What does *that* mean?"

"It means a pope. But a female pope."

"What's a pope?"

"It doesn't matter. It just means she's important like a queen or empress."

"A princess."

"No. A queen."

"Papesse *sounds* like princess."

"It does."

"What does she *do*?"

"She lays eggs."

"*Yuck!*"

"Thousands."

"*Ew.*"

"She mates with one of these fellows—" He points to the skittering mass of beetles.

"Fellows! Fellows? They aren't *fellows*! They are *beetles*!" Asthma screams. "And then what happens?"

"She incubates the eggs and then finds the right chamber somewhere under the log and she lays them, and then in due time a thousand, who knows how many, baby beetles hatch—"

"But *why*? I mean: why are they *here*?"

"Why is anything here? Why is anyone here?" With all the delicacy he can muster he touches her heart with his finger.

"Because I *want* to be." Asthma says it archly. "That's why, Mr. Brightfellow."

"Charter."

"*I'll* call you Brightfellow."

"I have far too many names as it is."

"When I name a thing it is the name it *needs* . . . Brightfellow. So there."

"You win."

"Tell me a story."

How beautiful the world is, he thinks as he sits down beside her on the grass, the beetles fully engaged in their affairs, and in the trees above them all manner of birds.

"Do you have anything in mind?"

"Make it up, Brightfellow, please. From scratch."

"There was once a planet," he begins, "made entirely—"

"—of *aspic.*"

"Of aspic. It was a frangible planet—"

"Frangible?"

"I mean to say feeble. Not really well enough to orbit the sun."

"It could not get too close to the sun, either."

"No, but it did. Each summer its elbow melted."

"Planets don't have elbows!" Asthma trills delightedly. "Planets don't have knees!"

"Planets made out of aspic have elbows and knees."

"Do they have people?"

"People who live their lives on place mats that float."

"Place mats! And they sleep under napkins."

"I have slept under worse things myself."

"Some look like saltshakers!"

"With heads like green olives. They are vociferous."

"Big word, Brightfellow."

"It means they talk all the time. Rather like you."

"Hmm." Asthma purses her lips in mock annoyance.

"And they are hirsute."

"Hmm . . . Brightfellow . . ."

"Which means they are covered with hair." Asthma shrieks. "And this . . . this *dismays* them." Asthma roars with laughter.

At this moment Blackie appears on the front stoop and her voice hatchets into the day like the voices of the birds that go: *Chirrup, CRACK! Chirrup, CRACK!*

"I have to go." Asthma knits her brows. "Blackie is taking me to the doctor." She stands and wipes the grass from the beautiful upended porcelain cups of her knees.

"Asthma!" Blackie shouts. "Who *is* that?"

"Brightfellow!" she shouts. "He's moved into the Old Fart's house across the street. He *lives* there!"

"Mind your language," Blackie shouts. "And move your ass over here, Asthma." Blackie waves at Charter. "Welcome to the neighborhood," she calls out, an afterthought, and walks to her car.

"I used to have a *tail*!" Asthma cries as she dashes off. "But I lost it in utero! *Now,*" she trills as she climbs into the car, "I have *worms*."

⬬

Although the sky is brighter than it has ever been, evening comes. From within the Circle's few squat screened radios, Ratmutterer's voice roaches:

I don't give a plucked hen, a plucked hen—if a faggot is a crackpot—if that dickhead doesn't swill beet soup. I don't give a scatophiliac's fig; he can percolate on an orange crate in front of the universe in his birthday suit, so what? But if he sucks begonias, I don't care if he's Woody Woodpecker or Minnie Mouse—he needs to be smashed with a hammer.

Once upstairs, Charter sees Asthma enter her room and begin to play with her town and its little animals. He thinks that if he could be at play beside her, he would recover all that is lost, all that was taken from him—so long ago now—when Jenny was sent away and all the games they had played together were reduced to the worst feeling of absence, with all the beauties of the world contained within that absence. Later, when he lies in bed, he recalls the long walk he took alone in the winter's snow to the madhouse on the hill. How he had asked for Jenny, had himself been asked for his name, his address. How the nice lady had asked, "Is Jenny not with you?" How when he walked to the door, sad and confused, he had seen the strangest-looking lady in the world pry her nostril with her tongue.

"Is she not with you? Is Jenny not with you?" This was how Jenny had been taken from him. Inexplicably and with a suddenness. When he had put the question to his mother, she had said: *Because.* Then, when pressed: *Because Jenny was beyond the pale.*

That night Charter dreams of the Hindu ascetic Cyavana, who was said to meditate within a hill of ants, fully submerged but for his eyes. Vanderloon writes that Cyavana's eyes burned like embers, *burned holes in the fabric of the days and the nights.* When Charter awakens to the smell of bacon he thinks it is time he finds himself a good pair of binoculars. His fork full of scrambled eggs, he asks Billy over breakfast if there is someone who teaches ornithology. There is. Professor Zim. Timothy. A good sort. Something of a bird himself, trim and quick. But why? *Owls,* Charter says. *There are so many. And the other birds. Much for study, I would think.*

After Billy goes off to "hunt and gather," Charter finds Dr. Zim's address in the phone book, and after a fifteen-minute canter descends into a lilac grove and sees the house, white with olive trim, quiet, unlocked. He makes the rounds before stepping into a small, cool kitchen as white as a hen's egg, its floors and counters gleaming. Everything in the house has a shine to it, is silvered with light, pristine. As he stands stricken with admiration in the kitchen, he thinks of all the many ways there are to live. The mole is happy underground, in its chamber carpeted with grass; the arctic fox dwells in mazes as vast as palaces; the weasel sleeps in deep hollows made by the roots of old trees; and the puffin will chase the rabbit from its den to claim it for himself. (There was a time in high school, before he ran off, when Charter read about different kinds of dwellings, and little else. He knows about the nests of wasps, the hives of bees, the places where the dung beetle hunkers down, the eagle, the carp. Writes Vanderloon: *The house is man's carapace, his pod, his shell, his coffin, or his cradle.*)

But! The house of the ornithologist! There are books, hundreds of them, each one jacketed in white paper, its title carefully inked on the spine. A small white plastic radio gleams on the spotless kitchen counter—also white—the walls are white and every single surface is level, alive with light, clear of clutter, accessible. There is not a single web, nor ball of dust; *there are no shadows!*

Charter steps over to the ornithologist's small refrigerator and pours himself a tall glass of orange juice. He drinks, rinses the glass, dries it carefully, and returns it to its shelf. And then he approaches the desk. It, too, is in order. There is a pale gray Olivetti with green keys, a stack of white paper, a clay mug full of sharpened pencils, a pen, and a bottle of ink. The ornithologist's house! Everything appears to be levitating and illuminated. Everything, that is, except for a very sturdy pair of binoculars—Brunchhausers! At a powerful 7 x 50. He lifts them by their strap from the back of a chair and slips them over his head. They thump against his heart. He stands empowered and alone in the kitchen, washed by the afternoon sun. It occurs to him that he has built his life from fragments belonging to others. From things stolen, lost, or abandoned. That he has cobbled together a life in the company of things devoid of any meaning beyond their utility.

That his life has no aesthetic unity. That there is no nobility to a life lived with such urgency as his, that he is no better than any hairy mammal carpeting its burrow with grass, and even now, in Billy's safekeeping, he is a dubious boy, and solitary.

Charter thinks that although Billy's house is perfectly accommodating, it has no uniqueness. Everything is replaceable, which is why it is an easy place for a serial interloper to set up shop. But the ornithologist's house! It *belongs* to the ornithologist! Just as it belongs to the instant, the instant that is eternal and serene—

Charter fears he is only a stargazer who sees light from things no longer there. The ornithologist lives in the light of the moment in a way unfamiliar to Charter, perhaps unknowable to him, and this is terrifying! For a moment he hears a chiming in his head, a familiar vortex of sound, and falls into a hole, the unfathomable hole that exists between one instant and the next.

Somewhere above him the springs of a mattress creak and then someone—the ornithologist!—is moving around upstairs. Charter leaps as from a dream and takes off, veering at once in the direction of a path that rises toward the road to campus. He picks up speed and runs easily, joyfully, the Brunchhausers knocking at his chest: they give him purpose, they give him weight.

Cyavana! thinks Charter as he runs. Cyavana! Cloaked in earth and swarming with ants, his eyes blazing . . . Vanderloon writes: *Cyavana in perfect disguise and isolation,*

*relentlessly transgressive as he gazes upon the world. His look-
ing is so like a hurricane in its intensity, it sends the world reel-
ing, and when that world comes to rest it is no longer the same.
It is irretrievably altered.*

—

Back at Billy's, Charter has taken up position in the shadows, the binoculars fixed to Asthma's window. Dressed in
a sheet, a peacock feather held to her temple with a bar-
rette, she has enchanted herself and wheels around the
tabletop like one possessed, setting up what appears to be
a parade.

Vanderloon divides mankind into two constants: the
ones who *know how to play, are full of mirth and fellow feeling,* and *the ones who are killjoys and combustible. Play,* he
writes, *is a powerful form of magic—sometimes white, sometimes black. But always it is born of invention and intuition.
Play is about becoming human, just as it is also about becoming a lion, a tugboat, a galloping stallion. The hallway that
leads away from the child's room and into the depths of the
house is a river, a glacier, a bridge to the moon.*

And now, the moment—and oh! it is prodigious!—
leaps into wonderment; Asthma is *making it snow.* She is
sowing fistfuls of silver confetti across the mirror lake, the
woods, the park, the barbershop and Sphynx, the brass
pyramid that—before it fell to the floor—was a cigarette
lighter. Charter feels this snow touch his hands and face

and knows the world is sacred. Space and time have dissolved, the window glass has dissolved. Charter and Asthma breathe the same air. Jenny beside them, using her scissors and glue.

He knows he will never get closer to life, that this moment is as close as he will get. The snow falls, star by star.

The smells of supper rise from the kitchen. Rich smells from a world light-years away. The radio is on and stupidly he thinks its sound travels at the speed of sound.

—

As Charter and Billy eat supper, Asthma talks to her toys. She says: "One understands animals. One understands because One *is* an animal. I know your hearts, my beloveds, and I know your minds. Because I, too, have an animal mind. Just the other day my intelligent friend Mr. Brightfellow said as much. Animals need a forest and they need a jungle. They need a varied and healthy diet, and a large number of bees are on their way, should arrive any minute, and they shall take over the bakery."

She ducks under the table and pulls out a white cardboard box. The box contains two dozen Chinese bees made of gauze and painted cotton. They have bright bead eyes and their little legs and feet are wire.

One by one she takes the bees out of their box and places them in front of the bakery, in rows of six. Then she introduces them to the cheering crowd, all up to their knees, bellies, necks, wings in snow. But someone—who can it be?—begins to make a rumpus. He fears bees! He loathes bees! *They are not animals! They fly around with daggers!*

"Who dares speak such nonsense?" Asthma demands that the heckler show himself. Who else could it be but the eternally grinning crocodile, who is forever sitting on a barrel when everyone else is walking around (except for the ducks, who cannot walk but remain swimming night and day). Asthma plucks him from the crowd and sets him down in front of the bees.

"Tell the crocodile why you have come all this way to celebrate First Snow and stay here with us forever and ever!" The bees begin to buzz and to hum. (If you looked very closely, you would see that each carries a tiny musical instrument—a harmonica, zither, xylophone, castanets, and so on. One holds a baton.)

"Honey!" the bees sing. "Bee cake. Royal jelly!" The bees sing in harmony. Their music *prestissimo*!

—

That night, as Charter lies awake, Dr. Ash prowls her yard. "I am losing my hair," she weeps quietly. "I am losing my mind." The breeze carries her voice directly to him. Charter likes to think this world of his is just one in an infinite set of worlds, each unique, some darker than others, some brimming with light. (He wants access to such a world!) Because these worlds are material, and because matter is driven to transform itself—just as a fox is driven to bite, just as a dreamy boy is driven to dream high dreams . . . Once a world begins anything can happen.

He considers Asthma, as he always does. She is uniquely beautiful and strange, mutable, unlike any other in this world or any other; he thinks that she will never reappear once her time is over, or if she does, she will be unrecognizable.

"I had a tail once!" She had said this so merrily! Perhaps there exists a parallel world in which another version of Asthma has kept her tail! A girl driven to thinking in riddles, who navigates the air, rising and falling like tumbleweed. He imagines a gilled girl, a celestial girl, a girl made of sound, a girl whose ribs cage the light.

The universe is immeasurable and so is a child's promise. Immeasurable. Today she wore a blouse printed with sea horses. She skipped down the middle of the street as the air billowed above her and he stood at the kitchen sink, spellbound. And now, alone in his study, her room still and dark, he is as lonely as he has ever been. He wonders if and when he will once more sit beside her, her very own Brightfellow! *Brightfellow,* she has named him. He backs away and falls onto the bed, having eaten a meal of impossible implications: not only meat and potatoes, but gravy and Parker House rolls—having paid his way with a fantastic tale of a swamp people who sleep and fish among the roots of trees; who milk the stars for answers to questions small and large; who dream of serpents; who know nothing of debt, of success, or even of failure; whose only punishment is silence; who see musical notation in the rotation of the planets; who know nothing of insomnia but instead sleep like hens. Whose infants are all born with yellow hair.

The room is uncannily still. Just as he begins to career into sleep, Dr. Ash's voice rises and for an instant he hangs suspended between two worlds.

"Ah!" She says it loudly. *"Rats."*

Just as sleep fully claims him, he idly wonders if his study might be made into a camera obscura, Asthma's window views magnified and projected onto his back wall. But why dream ways of seeing her if he has now entered so effortlessly into her world? Why not simply stroll past her yard again tomorrow?

That night he sleeps as does the clam inside its shell. One would need a knife to pry him open.

—

Meanwhile, Billy files his nails at the sink. Before Charter's arrival, he was in free fall. Now he bustles around with purpose. And Charter is brilliant, unexpectedly entertaining. What was it he had said? They sleep and fish among the roots of trees. They spend their lives in and around the water and never drown. That many are born albino . . . how mysterious! How marvelous!

But . . . what is that sound out by the Circle? Ah! It is Dr. Ash. What can possibly be wrong with her? Billy inspects his nails. They are perfect. But liver spots compromise the backs of his hands, hands that make him think of his wife. He is appalled that he had once touched her with pleasure. What could he possibly have been thinking? Better to caress an eel in the dark.

Outside, an owl whispers through the trees. And then everything is still, everyone sleeps . . . but not, not quite. Before the world goes silent, he hears Dr. Ash standing at her living room window and speaking. She is speaking to her house plant. "Why are you *so green?*" she asks. "Are you from *Mars?*" And she laughs.

—

"Brightfellow!" Asthma startles him. "What are you *doing?*"

Charter leaps to his feet. They are standing on a grassy embankment just above the pebble beach. The duck blind is leaping with flames.

"A small fire." He says it gently, his voice and manner warm, his eyes wild with something like euphoria. "Just a small fire." He pauses. "Asthma. Did you *follow* me?"

"You are not supposed to . . ." she answers evasively, and in confusion crouches beside him, her eyes on the flames.

"But isn't it beautiful," he says. "Do you see the blue roses, the black roses? And there," he gestures to the air in front of them. "See how the air is unsettled and shimmering. See how it seems to be melting? As if it were glass . . ."

"Yes!" She claps her hands. "It *is* melting! Fires always smell good," she decides.

"That's another reason why."

"Why?"

"Why I like them."

"Is this a secret?" she asks. In silence they look on as the fire builds. They listen to it crack and roar and then watch as it falls in upon itself, quiets. After a time all that remains is a small heap of embers." The air smells of burning leaves and branches, of scorched earth and canvas, of moss and mold roasting. Everything is heightened.

"Yes," Charter says at last.

"A fire," Asthma tells him with an intensity that stirs him, "is just like a kaleidoscope. It's always the same stuff moving around, and it's always different.

"Once I slept here," he tells her, "Oh, it was a while ago. In those days I was very much alone." He passes a stick of gum to her.

"I'm not allowed to chew gum," Asthma says. "May I have two?" She tells him she knows about a fox den nearby. Charter pushes the embers around with a stick to cool them, breaking up what is left burning.

"Show me," he says. He can see how the forest excites her. He can see that her hair needs washing and that her little cotton dress is stained with more than grass. He knows that in Blackie's house, much is left undone. When they reach the den and he peers in, it's the color of midnight. He smells fur. There are leaves and twigs scattered around, and one small bleached bone.

"Shh!" Asthma whispers just as he is about to speak. "She's sleeping now." He sees that she is flushed with excitement. Her knuckles are dirty and the little mole on her cheek is almost purple. This is the most beautiful day of his life. What *was* there to the world if not this?

"I don't have worms," Asthma tells him. And then with irritation, "Sometimes Blackie sees worms *everywhere*!"

●

"What was your day like?" Billy asks. He has served supper on the screen porch. A restful place, comfy. They sit in the early evening light, the smell of food from other houses mingling with that of Billy's curry. Rich as a kingdom, the table is studded with little bowls: peanuts, yellow raisins, toasted coconut, chutney. Charter is radiant; he has never been happier. He cannot stop smiling.

"Well!" Billy returns his smile. "You're in fine fettle."

"Yes! I am . . . in *fine fettle*!" The phrase tickles him and he begins to laugh. It is fortunate Billy joins him, because Charter cannot stop laughing. He is swept up in it. As the curry cools in their bowls the two of them roar with laughter.

All around the Circle people are at supper. The two Rods have set up a grill; Pea Pod is whining about her bloody portion of porterhouse, and Blackie is scolding Asthma, who has taken her baked potato and charred piece of meat up into a tree. Charter catches a glimpse of her bare legs and feet dangling from either side of a branch.

"Asthma!" cries Blackie. "Come down from there and *socialize*!" The houses are illuminated, houses filled with numberless things. What would it be like, Charter wonders, to grow up in a house with rooms filled with things so ordinary as to be invisible until the moment one reaches for them out of habit?

Billy stretches and sighs. "Is there any time of day better than twilight?" he wonders aloud.

"None! Look! Goldie's Rod is doing card tricks."

"Goldie's Rod. That's funny. Charter? What have you unearthed today?" He litters his curry with nuts.

"They have many names for wind."

"It's windy!"

"Always. All the time. The island is more or less thoroughly, ceaselessly, raked with wind."

"Raked!"

"Not a smooth surface anywhere. The vegetation is gnarled, hugs the ground; the leaves of things are small, hard as rubber. There is a plant, the Noola, that produces a large oily nut. They have to pound the shells with a heavy rock to break them open. They sing as they do this. They have songs for everything they do. They cook with Noola oil and rub their bodies with it. Everybody smells of Noola. They have a song for the moon's rising—"

"And for love?"

Charter blushes.

"You haven't told me all the names for the wind."

"Ah. Well . . . there is the wind that brings the flies—"

"Hah! Flies are a problem, then?"

"Only in season."

"And? I know! A Noola-whacking wind!"

"Yes. That too." Charter grins but for an instant fears he has been found out. But no; Billy continues:

"How good the air smells tonight. I wonder what it must be like to live among people who all smell like Noola! Does it get rancid?"

"You don't notice after a while."

"I had forgotten! You've *been* there!"

"Yes."

"Tell me!"

"It's a lovely, peaceable island where people never eat one another."

"For heaven's sake! Somehow it had not occurred to me—"

They sit on the porch for a time in silence. Night comes; it seems everyone around them has gone to bed except for Blackie, whose typewriter can be heard in the distance. Dr. Ash is nowhere to be seen; perhaps it is still too early for her to feel the full violence of her solitude. Only a cat moves in the grass.

"Puss! Puss!" Billy says to it. "Would you like a piece of curried fish?" But the cat ignores him and seeing something they cannot, dashes off after it.

"When autumn comes," Billy says, "I'll make cider. We'll go to one of the farms and bring back a carload of apples. How does that sound?"

"Thank you," Charter says, the full impact of his gratitude surging to his neck and face. Without thought he puts his hand on Billy's knee.

"None of that," says Billy, gently.

When Charter returns to his room, Asthma's window is dark. As dark as a fox hole is dark. *Shh,* Asthma had whispered. *She's sleeping.*

How vivid the day! Asthma, a wood sprite bounding and skipping beside him!

"Once I saw a cloud that looked like the face of a fox," she had told him. "Once a cloud just like an owl, and once just like my daddy's nose! It was exactly like his nose except it was a cloud!"

It is long after ten. The Circle is empty except for Goldie's Rod, who remains seated in his backyard nursing his rye. He is vaguely wondering about his teeth. He fears something is the matter with them. Perhaps he should make an appointment. Everything is so tiresome, so tedious. If only Pea Pod were an easier child to live with. And Goldie, too, is difficult. When they met he thought her handsome. He admired her heavy skeleton. She was clearly made to last. But now her size exhausts him. Living with Goldie is like living with a boa constrictor or a large piece of farm equipment. She's a tyrant, when you think of it, and when she sits down at the piano the world trembles.

Blackie's Rod is flat on his back, sleeping with his mouth open. Blackie lies beside him chuckling to herself. What would happen if she poured a thimbleful of Triple Sec down his throat? Once, briefly, she was with a man, a sculptor, who wore a long skinny braid down his back. When he abused her she left him, only to be plagued by an extended fantasy about cutting the braid off. She would make a clean cut at the nape of the neck. She would take care to dispose of the braid without leaving a trace. She imagined tracking him to a crowded restaurant. He would be drunk, engaged in an animated conversation. Everybody at the table would be animated, drunk. She would slip past, barely visible in an overcoat and a hat, her face concealed by a delicate web of veil. With a very sharp, small pair of scissors, she would cut the braid off and slip it into her coat pocket. She'd drift around a little as if looking for someone, and then she'd walk out the door. She'd find a garbage can on the street and drop in the braid. She'd continue on to her own favorite restaurant and order the clam linguini. She'd flirt with the owner, who, she knew, harbored a special weakness.

Suddenly she finds herself prodding her Rod. "Rod! Rod!" she cries. "Wake up, darling!"

"Why?" he mumbles and, turning, throws an arm over her. "Why do I have to?"

"Because," she says. "I've come to an important decision."

"Yes, Blackie," he mumbles. "Tell me quickly, will you . . ."

"We *must* find a way to have more fun. We *must*!"

Already he is fast asleep, his nose mashed up against her armpit.

Blackie imagines the sculptor would finish the evening unaware his braid is gone. At evening's end he would put on his overcoat, the one with the thick fur collar, and drive home. He'd peel off his clothes and tumble into bed. In the morning he'd take a shower. He'd reach for his braid to undo it and it would be gone. He would touch the back of his scalp first with one hand and then with the other. His palms flat against the back of his head he'd shout out a string of obscenities. He'd slam his fists together. He'd confront the inescapable.

—

That night Charter dreams he is a man made of paper. Lifted by the wind, he floats above a paper city, its windows, doors, bricks, and roof tiles all printed in colored inks. He wants to be dropped into the streets; he wants to wander among the shops and houses. But he is held suspended in the air without bone or muscle, a victim of the wind. He looks down at the city and calls out for help.

And then he gets his wish. He is dropped to the street and sees the walls of the city rise all around him. He wills himself to stand. But he is made of paper and can only lie on his back with the knowledge that sooner or later someone will step on his heart.

In the morning he sleeps in. There is a world of weight pressing down on him. Outside, the day is balmy and bright, a clear sky, a kind of sacred stillness until Blackie cuts loose—*I need a bigger theater than this!*—and Asthma, a screen door jangling behind her, dashes out of the house and into the cemetery. Just behind Dr. Swoboda's obelisk she nearly stumbles over Pea Pod who, on her knees, is packing a freshly made hole with indeterminate refuse. Pea Pod looks up at Asthma with terror.

"What are you doing? Pea Pod!"

"Shut your trap," Pea Pod implores her. "Mind your own business, Asthma!"

But Asthma is already poking around the hole.

"It's my hair." Pea Pod says it defensively. Asthma finds a tooth.

"It's *my* tooth," says Pea Pod. "All my teeth are there. Goldie keeps them. And my baby hair. I found this *box*. She keeps fingernails! Every time she cuts—"

Asthma is aghast.

"I'd *hate it*!" she tells Pea Pod ragefully. "If Blackie held onto, onto . . . my own body's *stuff*!" And she settles down beside her as Pea Pod finishes burying her hair, packing the top of the hole with earth. For a second they sit together behind the obelisk looking at the fresh spot of earth in the wet grass. Other than the birds, the cemetery is so still they can hear one another breathe. It is Asthma who breaks the silence. "What if *all* the mothers keep our bodies' stuff?" she whispers in horror, lamenting.

In the distance Blackie pounds away at *The Boy Beamed to Mars*.

•

A Sunday brunch on the lawn, Charter squirreled among the lilacs. Blackie's Rod does all the talking. He speaks and cannot stop speaking. Asthma is silent. Brooding. Silence fills her head like small bells, the kind sewn to woolen Christmas hats, ringing. A kind of tinnitus of the soul. The child, Charter thinks, will break away any minute. Unspool like a dervish, maybe ramble among the graves.

Blackie's Rod has his theories . . . at the moment he is attempting to prove that Michelangelo did not exist. Blackie knows he is compelled to deny the existence of genius because he is no genius himself. He loves smaller men. Puvis de Chavannes, for instance. A painter who never learned how to paint. If Puvis de Chavannes were alive today, he'd be designing labels for cold cream and chowder.

Blackie's Rod likes Senator Ratmutterer's courage. Ratmutterer, too, has no love of genius. Both hate the pretentious Hollywood crowd, whereas Blackie torments herself with envy for Ava Gardner, who at this very moment Blackie knows is having one hell of a good time. Her Rod likes to think he is related to Rusas, Chaldea's last king. A thing impossible to prove. He's going on and on about

Chaldea right now. Perhaps he speaks more intelligently about other things. It's hard to say. Hard to say because no one can listen to him for long. She thinks he is like a negative vessel. A sinkhole. Things getting sucked into him. Air, for example. The minutes of the day. The passing of the hours.

Suddenly Asthma leaps up with a small, irritated cry and dashes into the house. For the next hour he cannot track her down. What Charter does not know—no one does—is that there is a trapdoor in the attic that opens onto the roof. The roof is steep, shingled in slate, but she makes her way to the chimney and perches there. In a sea of branches, she has a full view of the Circle below. She sees Charter doing his funny thing among the lilacs, slipping in and out of the shadows. She has never understood why he doesn't just walk around like everybody else but, after all, Brightfellow is *not* everybody else! A small flock of crows break into the air above her; she gazes at them, excited by the closeness of their wings and bellies, their little feet. When she looks down, Charter is gone.

Just next door, Goldie's jewelry, scattered on the dresser, glitters. Charter pockets some loose change. These women remind him of his mother. Her vanity, her restlessness, her fistfuls of paste and glass. He thinks that someday they will walk out, just as his mother did. Their houses too small, their lives too small; even their children are too small! Perhaps for the first time he thinks of his mother's betrayal as the crime that eats up his life.

He knows the family is gone for the day and that he can take his time. Luxuriating, he rifles through Goldie's Rod's office. His coin collection is kept in heavy leather folders like talismans, and he has no idea as to their value, or how he can get money for them. But there is one thin little coin, possibly very ancient, stamped with a rooster-headed man with the tail of a snake. This he pockets, thinking: *Wonder is the first of the passions.* Was this . . . Descartes? Yes! The rest comes to him:

Wonder is a sudden surprise of the soul which makes it tend to consider attentively those objects which seem to it rare and extraordinary.

The room does not offer much else; he finds a cigar box packed with silver dollars and a very ugly pair of gold cufflinks tucked in the back of a file cabinet. This he takes along with a brand-new eraser—only because of its newness. That night he sleeps heavily, as if drugged, the coin beneath his pillow.

When he awakes his head chimes; yes, he awakens with a "chiming in the belfry," as he thinks of it, attempting to make light. He is pretty certain no one else walks around submerged as he is in such a clatter. When he enters the kitchen he finds a note; Billy has a dinner plan involving a *plateau de fromages,* a thing he recalls from frequent summer visits to France back when he was married—*such a mistake that was!*—to a woman who did not travel well, who could not manage her wine, and who loathed cheese. Once, served lamb kidney, she shrieked! A woman who could not stomach the sound of foreign languages, but who had been beautiful, *built like a boy with the thighs of a boy and the sweetest bottom!* All this Billy had revealed the night previous as once again they sat together on the screen porch, the crickets sounding all around them, the locusts and the occasional owl, the air fragrant with the smells of freshly mowed grass and carried by the soft breeze of a deepening spring. The screen porch was divine, waiting for Charter as he wished, his eyes wandering his domain. *With the sweetest bottom . . . but when she laughed, oh . . . when she laughed! I came to hear the mule, the jackal, the raven . . .*

Billy. Already Charter cares for Billy. In the first days he thought of him as the "Old Boy," the "Old Fag," but now it's *Billy*, wistful, generous, trusting (!), clueless (thank god!), dependable—already he knows this—Billy. The note—*Off on a cheese run!*—left on the counter.

Charter makes himself toast. His head clear, his heart calm. He is focused yet somehow relaxed; there is a new ease to his body, his entire manner. Billy has noticed this and is pleased to see Charter fits in his clothes, moves with a certain grace. He has provided Charter with shirts, *beautiful* shirts from years before when, full of hope, he took his wife to Normandy, the Val de Loire. They have been carefully washed, ironed, and folded by his vanished wife. A new pair of khakis has shown up in a locker in the gym and Charter has spent some of his pilfered cash on undershirts and socks. A bottle of Old Spice.

He has been thinking that he should ask Goldie's Rod how to do card tricks. He must do a better job entertaining his host tonight. Billy, a linguist with a special fascination for Romance languages, French above all. *A language!* Charter considers. Plucked as it were from the birds. Not only their voices, but their tracks in wet sand, the shapes of their beaks, the markings on their bellies and backs; a language painted on bark that looks like bird tracks (the birth of cuneiform? The tracks of bird feet on the wet mud by the riverside?); a people who cry out to one another like herons . . . yes! He must make this island he is inventing really *shine*. He climbs the stairs to his study.

Asthma. Asthma in the glass! A grain of sugar in his eye. Today she is leaping around like a colt from the floor to her bed, bed to floor, floor to bed, then dashing through the house. Her feet are bare and her spare cotton dress billows like petals around her small frame. When he hears the front door slam he gets up to find and follow her. But when he hits the Circle she is simply in the front yard beside the beetle log, poking at it with a twig.

"So where *are* they, Brightfellow?" she asks.

"They live eventful lives."

"They're *beetles*, Brightfellow. They live in a *log*!"

As she speaks, Charter relishes the proximity to her skin, her little ears, her impossible eyelashes, a vague smell of piss, of violets. He thinks she is oblivious to her beauty, which is like a flame. He thinks, *This is what angers Blackie. This flame.* He says:

"There's a labyrinth under that log."

"No there isn't."

"There's a treasure at its farthest end." She looks up at him eagerly, expecting a story.

"Every lost ring, every lost earring, every lost button, each and every time a stone falls from Blackie's sapphire brooch—"

"How do you know—"

"Because I see her wearing it sometimes when she walks over to Goldie's for cocktails."

Asthma snorts.

"Every time a pearl necklace comes undone and a pearl rolls under the piano—"

"They find it!"

"They find it and carry it between their teeth to their Queen."

"Brightfellow." Asthma furrows her brow and, folding her arms across her chest, says: "Beetles don't have *teeth*. And she's not a queen. She's a *Papesse*. Don't you remember *anything*?"

"A Papesse. Exactly. She sits in her chamber bedded down in one of your lost mittens, surrounded by all the things that we have lost."

"How boring is *that*?"

"That's not the end of it." Asthma frowns and looks at him with a certain ferocity. She has a restless mind, and sometimes he wonders if he has met his match. "She craves far better," he tells her. Asthma nods and moves closer. He notices how the sweet bones of her fingers come together as she hugs her knees.

"There's a beetle. A green one. Named 'The Finder.'"

"Because finders keepers!" Asthma approves. "He's the one who finds this stuff!"

"Yes. He uses it for barter. The Papesse has no interest in Blackie's fake sapphires."

"They're not *fake*!"

Charter raises an eyebrow knowingly and looks at her with amusement.

"How do you know they are FAKE?"

"Hush," he says. "Asthma—I have my ways." He continues: "The Papesse has no interest in silver dollars or wedding rings inscribed with the word *Forever*."

"Beetles can't read. But what *does* she want? Tell me." She pokes Charter hard in the thigh with her finger. "Come *on*, Brightfellow."

"She wants a certain *key*."

But before he can say more, Goldie appears, wheeling toward them in platinum sandals, Pea Pod in tow, and they are *formally introduced* (Asthma's words), and Asthma is being told to play with Pea Pod in her room for an hour or so because Goldie simply must get to town.

"I'll look after them," he says. "I'll take them birding." And he flashes his binoculars.

—

His pulse quickens as the three of them set off together into the woods behind Asthma's house and into the little cemetery.

"Look, Brightfellow!" Asthma leads him to a spot behind a familiar pink granite gravestone, one that has in the past provided him many long hours of concealment. "I buried a mole here. Don't tell Blackie. She says it's . . . I'm . . . *macabre*." Turning, she points to an upstairs window. "I can see the exact spot where I buried it from my bedroom. It had *fangs*!" Charter shudders. They are standing just a foot away from one of his best vantage points in the gravestone's shadow.

And then she takes his hand.

"Brightfellow," she says. "Tell us about the key."

"I don't *want* to hear about a silly old key!" Pea Pod whines. He notices how her eyes don't quite match up, her expression somehow skewed, but he cannot put his finger on what it is that troubles him. Only eight years old, he thinks, and the child is already coming undone at the seams.

"The beetles in my yard," Asthma ignores her, "have a special key. Brightfellow has seen it."

"That's stupid." Pea Pod is scratching at a scab. She works her scabs with diligence. The air around them swims with the sounds of locusts rising and falling and rising . . .

"The key is to a laboratory," Charter persists, "deep beneath the earth. And it is here, in this secret laboratory, that precious things are made and astonishing things happen."

"Precious things," Pea Pod muses, suddenly mollified. "Like dollies."

"Dollies!" Asthma snorts.

"Better than that. Things like . . . cinnabar. Which is a kind of scarlet sand you can find in the cliffs above the river. The ants love it—no one knows why—and grain by grain carry it in their jaws to a hidden place beneath their hill. Once inside, they grind the sand down to a fine powder and then they wash it in a copper bowl—copper, too, they manufacture, no one knows how—and then they wash it again."

Now the air is charged with a vivid interest from Asthma and Pea Pod both. They are sitting on a large flat stone that leans out above the woods below. Asthma and Pea Pod sit side by side, at peace with one another.

"Then they go to sleep," he continues. "And when they wake up the cinnabar has settled at the bottom of the bowl. They drain off the water and allow it to dry. It's now a bright scarlet of great depth and beauty. The Papesse—"

"Is *red*!" Asthma chimes, wildly excited. "Pea Pod! She's *red*!"

"Exactly so!" Charter musses Asthma's hair affectionately. "How very quick you are, Asthma. So . . . now do you know why she is so beautiful and why she needs the key?"

"Not really."

"Here's why. The ants knead the cinnabar with soft beeswax into a paste . . ."

"I don't understand what you are talking about!" Pea Pod shouts and, in a rage, scrambles to her feet. "I want to go home!"

"Don't ruin it, Pea Pod!" Asthma cries, leaping up. "I bet the beetles *wax her*, Pea Pod! Like you wax a piano!" She doubles over with laughter. "Right, Brightfellow? They *wax her*? They *wax her*!" she says, barely able to get the words out.

"But what about the *key*?" Pea Pod cries, on the verge of sobbing. "What about the *key*?"

"It doesn't matter!" Asthma is out of patience. "Obviously they use the key to get into the laboratory to steal THE RED WAX!"

"Who? WHO?" Pea Pod screams. "WHO NEEDS THE KEY?"

"THE BEETLES!" Asthma shouts. "GODDAMNIT, Pea Pod!"

"The ants make a paste," Charter explains gently. "They roll it into little balls the size of peas and put it in a cabinet. The cabinet is locked. When the ants go to sleep, the Papesse sends her butler—"

"Not her *butler*," Asthma complains. "It can't be her butler. It has to be her . . . her . . . I don't know what!"

"You're fast, Asthma," Charter says. "He's called the butler—and you'll see why—but in fact he's a footman, and like all beetles he has sticky feet. Once he's snuck into the laboratory and opened the cabinet, he collects the balls of cinnabar with his sticky feet and then he carries them to the Papesse. Who has been waiting for him all night long impatiently. Because her color is fading and she needs him to—"

"WAX HER!" Asthma exults. "See? Pea Pod? WAX her all over!"

"Which is why he's called 'the butler,'" Charter interjects triumphantly. "It's his way of dressing her. He's also called: the *Butterer.*"

"It's not a story!" Pea Pod screams. "IT'S NOT A STORY! Let's go to your room! Like Goldie said we were *supposed to.*" She stomps off.

"I'm staying here with Brightfellow," Asthma says, pressing a little square of pink bubble gum into the palm of his hand. "The *Butterer.*" She smirks.

•

The philosophers warn us that our perceptions are not to be trusted, yet we must assume that the mother is soused when she slurs her consonants, that the child is making fudge when the heavy copper pot is brought out and set on the stove. And it is a fine thing when our perceptions pan out. As when Asthma appears at Billy's door with that very fudge, still warm, and the next thing you know, you're sitting on Blackie's lawn between two little girls smelling of summertime, eating fudge with your fingers.

It is Saturday; the sound of ice tumbling from freezer trays shatters in the air. And here is Goldie, gin and tonic in hand, dressed to the nines, her face painted within every inch of its life, and with a plan for the rest of the afternoon. She will take us to town for a movie, the girls and I will have our supper at the soda fountain. (Cheers at all this.) After, Goldie will fetch us and bring us all home. She's footing the bill, she assures me.

The impossible unfolds. We are in Goldie's car. We are leaving the Circle, driving past the library, the empty classrooms, the outlying woods—and then the road is flanked for long minutes by trees—the clam shack, gas station, Annie's next; the little houses painted white and green. The scarred place where my father's house once stood. Farmland and then Hawkskill, its grocery, its five-and-dime, its bar, and the very heart of downtown. And we are walking into the Moonlight Theater. I am handing our tickets over to a boy who tears them apart. I am buying Tootsie Rolls, overseen by a brass sphinx and an eighth-grader in braids, then guiding the girls past a plaster obelisk carved with dismembered feet and hands, sacred ladders, pancakes, and birds. We are treading the Moonlight's indigo carpet, a carpet swarming with *putti* and stained with root beer. Sitting at last in the blue shadows, the girls at each of my elbows, taking in a shimmering red curtain, watching it part like something melting away, watching the stars orbit the mountain, the rabbit chomp his carrot and evade death; watching Jimmy Stewart, his binoculars so like my own, his habits so familiar. I sit on my little velveteen upholstered chair, fully realized: a designated guardian of

little girls! And here is the irresistible Jimmy Stewart immobilized by a broken leg, just as I've been immobilized by a
broken whatever-it-was that was broken! My soul was it?
My mind? I sit as happy as I believe I was intended to be,
as the girls ferret in their pockets for Tootsie Rolls and Wax
Lips without once looking away from the screen.

Later, over toasted cheese sandwiches and vanilla milk-
shakes, the girls discuss the movie. They both disapprove of
Jimmy Stewart's nipples—"men should not *have* nipples!"
(Asthma); "no one should have nipples!" (Pea Pod). They
wonder about the logistics of cutting up a body and taking
it out the door one piece at a time. They suppose the thighs
look like hams and that there would have only been room
for two in the suitcase. They wonder if the knees would
have been attached to the thighs. They think it unjust the
dog was murdered. "It was not a whiner" (Pea Pod). "It
was the *wife* that whined" (Asthma). She turns to me, says,
"Jimmy Stewart reminds me of you."

"But I don't have nipples," I manage.

"Looking out that window, stupid," she says.

"We all do that," I tell her. "That is what windows are
for." I make a strange noise in spite of myself, something
like a frog being strangled.

"You do so have nipples!" Pea Pod says ragefully. "Everybody does! It doesn't make any sense!" She decides.

"I like spying," says Asthma.

"She spies on you!" cries Pea Pod, sloppily sucking foam
from the bottom of her glass with a straw. And then, as the

earth heaves under me, she adds: "He's a peep peep, peep peep, peeping Tom" to the tune of "Sh-Boom."

On the way home, Goldie, looking flushed and pawed over, asks Asthma what she wants to be when she grows up. Without hesitation she says:

"I want to be a pickpocket."

"You are one hell of a tease," says Goldie.

"I want to be a mermaid," Pea Pod, wearing Wax Lips, whispers incomprehensibly.

"Asthma is speaking cryptically and symbolically," I say, having regained my composure. "What she is saying is she wants to see the beauties of the world and live her life deeply." Asthma snorts.

"Since when," snarls Goldie, "do eight-year-olds need interpreters?"

—

The Époisses is pungent, it raises a stink. Charter holds his breath and takes a bite. It tastes of the forest floor, mushroom maybe, the underside of a rock. It's fecund, impossibly rich, and it is *good,* astonishingly so when eaten with crusty bread and wine. There is also a Maroilles—equally fetid, outrageous, maybe even obscene, delicious. For the first time Charter tastes a Côtes du Rhône. *This,* he thinks, *is the life.*

The Époisses thickening his tongue, Billy mumbles: "Tell me more about the—what did you say they were called?"

Bloody hell . . . the wine. The wine! Charter can no longer remember.

"The Mannja . . . Mannja . . . ," Billy struggles.

"The Mannja Fnadr." Charter recalls it. "Let's see; well: when it thunders—and it thunders often—they strike things together, things like bones or stones. This is done to remind the gods that they, too—the Mannja Fnadr— can *make a noise*."

"And when they die?"

"They say when it's time to die, the gods pull them up to the sky by the neck with something like a fishhook."

Billy roars with laughter. Charter joins him and for a moment they are both once again overcome with hilarity. But just as quickly Charter is sickened by this laughter. He feels he has betrayed—and how absurd this is!—these people, the Mannja Fnadr, whom he has invented! He thinks he must come up at once with a transcendent vision. He wants the Mannja Fnadr to impress Billy. He wants them to forgive him for his banalities, his facile mocking of their "savage" state!

"And the *soul*?" Billy asks, as if reading his mind. "What do they say of the soul?"

"They say . . . they say we each have a bird within us. A bird of breath, a bird of fire. Longing for . . . release." Billy grows quiet all at once and his gaze clouds over.

"Longing," Billy says. "Yes. For release. Yes. Yes! That's *it*, isn't it! What we all—"

"I never told you what Mannja Fnadr means," Charter continues. "It means *the first ones here*. And they may well be. The first ones to come; the first ones with sinew in the soul."

"Such a notion, Charter: sinew in the soul. Why that's downright wonderful!"

"It also means: *first sprouting* or, if I understand correctly, *first budding of the initial impulse.*"

"My god! My god!" Billy rises, agitated, and begins to pace. Earnestly he says: "I sometimes wonder, cannot help but wonder, what if we—yes our entire species—are the *first budding,* the first and only, Charter! And what if we've . . . *missed the boat?*"

The early evening has moved closer to the night. In this way, eating and speaking together, they live the hours. In a brief week's time, on such a night as this, Billy will ask Charter: "Tell me something of your father's death. You carry it awfully close to your heart, I can tell. You said your mother had gone far too soon, but peacefully, but what of your father?"

Charter will not see this coming and he will be knocked off balance. What had happened to his father had been terrible. Charter could not tell Billy how he had run away, been homeless, a scavenger, living under porches, in cabinets stocked with dead mammals floating in formaldehyde—all that. How he had returned one day to find his father on the floor, how his father had been dead well over a week, how he had built a good fire in the middle of the house, how that fire had brought it all down, everything down to ashes. Instead he will say: "A long illness. A long and terrible illness." Which in its way was true.

It is late. Outside, Dr. Ash is wandering in her yard. "It's all wrapped up!" she shouts, startling them. "Wrapped up and posted!"

"I have no child," Billy says. "The house, as you know, belongs to the college, but everything in it, what I have in the bank, well—it will all go to you. Do not protest. I have thought this over carefully. I have thought of little else for some days now."

—

After Billy goes up to bed, Charter returns to the porch. Wearing a towel and barefoot, Dr. Ash is not far, her voice more or less carried by the breeze. *Dearest . . .* she murmurs. *Dearest . . . my dear heart.* There is a good breeze moving through the leaves and as it lifts the night is replete with voices. *Dearest,* she says. *Dear heart . . . my dearest heart.* He hears the cat, the crickets, the owl, the fleet passage of something or other; he sails the night on a sea of sound. Dr. Ash says: *I shall make an inventory*—and off she goes.

For a time hers is the only light remaining. Everyone is on their backs adrift in the night. As he sits there alone on the porch, things continue to spill past like smoke—the wood, after all, is close at hand. A fox perhaps, or hedgehog. The Circle is now theirs. He imagines this must be a relief. Their beautiful unhindered nights, the air alive with bats and fireflies, crickets, moths, things with fur, owls.

But then he catches her scent; it is Asthma, Asthma breathing just behind the screen.

"Brightfellow!" she whispers. "Dr. Ash is scratching around in the cat box!"

"No! No!" Charter leaps to his feet, startled. Horrified. "That can't be!"

"It *could* be true, though."

"Don't upset me like that, Asthma."

"Blackie fell asleep on the couch."

"Go put a blanket on her, Asthma, dear. It's a chilly night." This appears to pain her. But as much as he adores, yes, *adores,* her proximity, he is unsettled by this unexpected intimacy. Panic rises within him. So he says, "I'm turning in."

"Good night, Goodfellow," Asthma breathes, her nose pressed to the screen. "Good night, *gadabout*"

But Charter does not turn in. And now, alone on the porch in the dark, he is dismayed that he *sent her away*! Asthma, right there behind the screen, *a breath away*, gleaming! Asthma! Her breath a secret writing on the air. She surges in his mind's eye, tucked into a bed littered with animals, crayons, books, her pajamas buzzing with planets, moons, stars. Her window as dark as the ink of squids, the deepest recess of deepest space.

He realizes for the first time—how has this escaped him?—that the houses on the Circle are *all the same*! Except for the way they are placed at odd angles, each with a different approach. The houses orbit the Circle, as it were, the one tugging at the other. The weather all around them ebbing and rising—a network of sighs and bewilderments.

And their windows are like eyes.

Loon, quoting one of the ancients, wrote that the white objects that shine within the eyes are engendered by white atoms, and the black objects are borne of a black seed. Charter falls asleep thinking that objects *seed the eye*—a lovely idea—and dreams he has made an observatory out of cardboard and paper and that it fits the Circle, illuminated by the moon. He takes Asthma by the hand and leads her around the perimeter. Asthma says: *I want to look inside,* and kneeling, peers into a hallway that leads straight to the big dome and its telescope. Looking into the telescope she sees her own face painted on the moon. *Oh, Brightfellow!* she says. *Now you've gone and done it again, Brightfellow!* And Charter knows he has "done it again" and this knowledge is terrible. But what it is he has done again he cannot say. *Now you have done it again!* He hears Asthma's voice as he awakens before dawn, chilled to the bone and damp with dew. He goes inside for a shower, the dream hot in his mind, his head once again ringing. Oh, he is alive with bells. As when, years ago now, he had returned home after a long absence, and found his father there on the floor in a heap, the gentle man he had not seen much of when he had sold seeds; Charter had seen too much of the other one, broken and ghostly, who installed toilets.

The doubled father, seeded black, and seeded white, who had been—with everything around him—reduced to ashes because it had seemed at the time the one and only thing that Stub could do, should do. A great big cleansing fire.

As Charter showers, Billy stirs. He hears the water running and then falls back asleep. Just as Charter gets into bed, the sun rises, Billy reawakens, and as always the somewhat incomprehensible moments unfold. Billy is aware of the slightest thorning of his heart, which he imagines is something like a tiny prick of the thinnest pin, thinner even . . . and he is aware of his nausea—this also slight; he is anxious, and this despite the presence of the boy—the boy, Charter—who (at last!) assures him a place on a planet that spins, a place to stand firmly and feet to walk as others do, without question—or so he supposes—except that today, as Charter sleeps deep into the morning, he is full of questions again. Perhaps this is all about the fact that he is on his third cup of coffee, or the fact that the sky is growing quickly darker, a thunderstorm is rolling in and the darkness, the taste of metal in the air recalls his marriage, a marriage in which—or so it seems to him now—he was often to blame for something or other. And he *was* to blame, after all, for a wife who had not been what he had actually wanted, when you got down to it. The young men were what quickened him, above all the young clerk at the small family-run shoe store, with whom he had once talked about the merits of a pair of oxfords. Billy had asserted that the shoes were not quite the right size although the clerk—Billy did not dare ask his name—the clerk who smelled of bitter almonds told him they were perfect, just right; they fit like a dream. He has never forgotten the feel of the clerk's two hands on his heels, his ankles, how he looked on, captivated, as the laces were tugged and tied. He bought them, of course, the oxfords! And kept them in their box—a talisman, the clue to an essential memory, the emblem of his longing, the sinew of his soul. He never once wore them.

As the first of the rain needles the windows, Billy thinks that if they fit, he will give the oxfords to Charter. Charter will wear them and they will enable him to somehow step into his own life. An insane idea, perhaps, but Billy embraces it. *It is too late for me,* he thinks. But for Charter the world has only just begun.

—

By the time Charter descends into the kitchen, Billy is gone, gone to Kahontsi to meet with his lawyer. Billy is happy. Something important has been solved.

The day is dark, chilly—unusually so; there is rain. Looking out the front door, Charter sees Dr. Ash at her upstairs window, her mind brimming with numbers and strange ideas. He knows she is considered a genius; he has seen numbers tattooed on her wrist but does not know their significance, supposes they are emblematic of her profession. His brilliant mind is riddled with lacunae such as this. The chiming in his head is dizzying; he reverberates. His soul's metal is hammered to within an inch of its life and he is cold. *Soon it will be fall*, he thinks, although it is only June. Trembling, he decides to build a fire; there is nothing to do but build a fire.

There are no logs by Billy's fireplace, so he goes down to the basement, where he finds stacks of cardboard, the *Ohneka Tribune*, and a few old orange crates. He makes logs of cardboard and paper rolled together and tied with string, breaks up the crates, and constructs a fire, setting the logs down on top of the kindling. He spills kerosene liberally and lights a match, then watches as the entire structure bursts into flame. It's beautiful! But the damned thing starts to roar and smoke floods the room. Charter is at a loss; smoke fills his nose, his eyes; and the mantel is smoking, sizzling! The map of France hanging above it cracks and glass rains down.

Charter dashes to the sofa, grabs a pillow, and shoves it into the hearth; he grabs another, then a third. Runs into the kitchen for a basin of water and sends it cascading into the mess. The room smells like smoke, toasted rayon, and chicken feathers. He sits down on the couch, devastated.

"You've really done it now," says Asthma, coming into the room. She sits down next to him. "Everybody knows these fireplaces are pretend." Then, quickly, breathlessly, she leans to his ear and says: "Dullfellow. My best-ever friend."

There is no way out of this dilemma, no way to explain it. Agitated, pale, Charter dashes up the path as soon as he hears Billy's car. Asthma is there also, bouncing with excitement.

"Something terrible has happened!" Charter cries, clearly distraught. "Something *terrible*!"

Billy, deeply concerned, embraces Charter, says, "My boy! My boy! What has happened?"

"Fire!" Asthma explodes. "But we caught it in time! Didn't we, Brightfellow?"

Billy enters the living room, sees the damage to the fireplace, the map of France, the ceiling blackened with smoke—the mess on the floor where the scorched pillows have left a mark.

"It is amazing," Billy says with good humor, "when you think of it, that this has not happened before. It is irrational, *irrational*—like so much in our world—to build a fireplace that cannot hold a fire! It's o.k., Charter. I'll give a call to Buildings and Grounds and we will get on with what remains of the day." He bends over and pecks Asthma on the cheek, says, "You have spunk. I do appreciate that in a child."

"I'll replace the pillows," Charter begins, but Billy stops him, says:

"You have better things to do with your insignificant allowance than provide me with pillows!"

—

When the mornings are lazy, the coffee thoughtfully prepared, the conversation cheerful and already leaning into dinner, one's shirts pulled hot from the dryer, the refrigerator ample with orange juice and cottage cheese—well then the days are effortless, effortless the hours, and Charter begins to let go, to take things as they come, to take things in. He dares believe there is a place for him. He dares believe he is not so strange after all.

A merry band of men in overalls undo the damage to Billy's living room. Windows are washed, sheets changed. The lawn has never been greener. The lilac never more fragrant. Billy and Charter go into town to hunt down sofa pillows. There is a lunch in a gracious white inn with a view of the water. Roast-chicken sandwiches made with thick house mayonnaise and pickles.

"Billy!" Charter begins, "This sandwich is—"

"Isn't it! Charter, dear boy! *Isn't it!*"

The two take their ease, companionable, happy. For the first time Billy speaks of his teaching, his passion for the French poets: *the cell of myself fills with wonder . . . the white-washed walls of my secret . . .*

"What is his secret?" Charter wonders aloud.

"He's speaking of the deeper self, I think. The one we embodied when we were little children. When we could reinvent the world undisturbed."

"For days at a time," Charter whispers. "As outside the snow falls hour after hour."

"Yes. That is it. Exactly . . . I had a student once," Billy says, "who translated Jouve brilliantly. He died the night he graduated, stupidly, in the river—although he knew how to swim. The entire campus mourned for months."

On the way home, Charter dwells on the loss of the young man. The faculty and students mourning together as one moves him deeply. And he feels the familiar pang of loss, feels the old longing to have lived in this place as those students did, the place he had abused—yes, this is the word that comes to him—and is abusing still. He fears it is because he is twisted, he is strange. Sitting in the comfort of the car, the windows open to the day's benevolence, Charter feels the full force of this chronic strangeness once again.

After they return, Charter spends what remains of the afternoon wandering the campus he knows so well, yet not at all. He recalls the many times he has sat on the grass in the sweet nights of Indian summer once classes had begun, listening to chamber music spelling the air around the chapel, or the sound of someone playing a horn, a piano, in the little music studio tucked away in a grove of pines. Such things he recalls . . .

In all those years he only once dared step into a class-room. When the professor asked his name he fled. And once he dared creep into the theater, crouched in the wings, watching the rehearsal of a play. He recalls now the pain of that moment, a feeling of such isolation it had been almost untenable. Fearful of discovery, he had remained frozen in the shadows for hours, so crushed by the weight of his own singularity he could barely stand after everyone was gone. He had unfolded his limbs like a crushed Jack rising from a rusty box. Making a terrible joke at his own expense, he had sputtered between his teeth: *Screek! Screek!*

Now, approaching the Circle, he thinks: *I must find a way to be—to be what? True to life. Real.* Why was it so hard? It was impossible. Insurmountable. He was an impostor through and through, a coward and a liar. He was one hell of an evasive, secretive, spooky sonofabitch!

In the early light of evening, the campus is resplen-dent. Somehow unfathomable, so much grander than his own aspirations. Aspirations? Has he aspirations? He who is living such a small life, something cramped and reduced (how is this possible?) despite the promise this place pro-vides him to live out a wealth of dreams? Yet here he is, as always, on the perimeter of that promise, soaking up a lonely man's many kindnesses, embroiled in the frustra-tions of the soused faculty wives and their brats—but no! It is not as simple as that! Because . . .

Watching Asthma. Those transcendent moments when everything dissolves and something epic takes over, something coherent, a thing that again and again surpasses itself. The moments surpassing themselves—as once, when he was a tiny child, his father had opened his little valise and one by one taken out the packages of seeds and taught him the names of things.

—

Much later, long after Billy has gone to sleep, Charter once more dozes off on the screen porch. He awakens to the sound of Dr. Ash wandering and is afraid that if she ever wandered away and was forever lost, the Circle would be intolerably still. As she passes in the shadows not far from him, he understands that all it would take is a few small steps from the porch to the yard to find her. And so he does this, he takes those steps, and as soon as he does, Dr. Ash stops her pacing and stands perfectly still. And he finds that he is holding her, that she is holding him. They cling to one another for dear life. Silently, she begins to cry, her tears spilling from her eyes like rain. The front of his shirt is wet where her face presses against his chest.

After a time she lets her arms fall, and stepping back, her hair clouding her face, smiles at him. It is a moonless night but the sky has a glow. He sees this smile of hers and returns it. Thank you, she says, turning away, waving once with a sweet, small gesture of her hand. Off she glides; he hears her enter her dark house, sees her move through the house as she illuminates it room by room; he stands there alone taking this in, strangely moved, a profusion of blue shadows and lustrous scents pressing around him.

Dr. Ash is beautiful. But Charter is desireless; desire is a thing unknown to him. In some vague way he thinks the best lives are somehow disembodied, suspended . . . not bruised by imperious need or weakened by the renouncements of day-to-day living. Perhaps Dr. Ash shares this idealism. Maybe idealism is the place from which she stands, scorched and lonely. Not without desire, clearly— *Beloved*, she had said the other night, *my dearest heart.* But her desire has become idealized—or so he imagines—a perfect thing, perhaps too perfect to endure. (Of course he knows nothing of what she has endured. He does not know, cannot know, that she was speaking of a child.)

—

The world is a riddle, quarreled and tormented. It is threaded through with darkness, or, worse, its fabric is dark through and through. Rarely does a bright thread work its way into the weave.

He retires early. He takes the coin out from under his pillow and gazes at it for a long time. It is an unsettling thing, as old as time, he thinks. Yes. It's like holding a small slice of time between his fingers. Made of copper yet with the weight of lead. Its unsettling little figure is familiar; looking at it now he feels an old malaise. And then he recalls a drawing of Vanderloon's that had served as a frontispiece for *Rules of Rage,* his most disquieting book. A book so disquieting Charter had never managed to finish it.

He decides he must rid himself of the coin at once. He pulls on some clothes and slips into the night, walking in the deepest shadows until he reaches the woods beyond the library, and there, finding two good stones, hammers the coin between them, smashing it to bits. After, he returns to Billy's and sleeps, but the little coin continues to exert some influence, or so he fears, and he thinks he must undo this nefarious influence by taking something of Asthma's—an animal from her tabletop town. He will replace the coin with one of the many creatures she rules over with such devotion. He begins to watch her house differently, like a man in a fairy tale whose life depends upon a treasure he knows is just within reach. But the weather turns—thunder and all the rest—and everyone is caught in place. Asthma in her room, Blackie at her typewriter, and Blackie's Rod glued to his stamp collection.

●

He is weary. He has been watching for too long and has torn open a can of worms. He is fractured and leeched. Because today, as he stands in the shadows, the ornithologist's binoculars burning his eyes, he sees Pea Pod and Asthma at play—an enigmatic game that involves scolding and finger wagging; it involves shouting. Something savage is unfolding, savage and absurd. It is as if Blackie and Goldie are straddling the rafters and tugging at their offspring's strings.

The game intensifies and accelerates. The girls are shouting with such force their voices carry across the Circle and into the woods. He sees Pea Pod raise her fist in the air, throw herself at Asthma, and pummel her heart. He sees Asthma slap Pea Pod across the face with such force Pea Pod stumbles and falls, vanishing as if swallowed by the floor—only to rise again and fly at Asthma and, like a wild thing released from its cage, bite her arm.

Charter turns away. Repulsed and despairing, he falls to his knees, his hands held to his ringing ears. When an instant among the many rises above all the rest to seize the mind, what are the consequences? He shivers. He has seen something primal, grotesque. He has seen two little girls transformed into harpies before his eyes.

Or maybe not. Maybe he is overly sensitive. Overly concerned. Perhaps little girls, just like little boys, inflict these punishments on one another thoughtlessly, in the spirit of play, with no ill intention. In childhood he was never in a scuffle; he would watch other boys bewildered, their passions inscrutable, given to an animal impulse. Like the hissing of kittens. After all, he knows his Asthma. Knows her tender ways. Knows her sweetness, the innocence with which she took his hand, whispered in his ear . . .

—

It's Sunday. Billy and Charter relax with bowls of café au lait and the *Ohneka Tribune*. The calm is breached by shouting: a child howls, then another. The scene that haunts him infects another hour. *Muzzle her!* Goldie screams. *Pea Pod! Little thief!* Billy leaps from the sofa and closes the windows. "It never stops!" Billy mutters, "I think it's getting worse." Moments later the doorbell rings. Charter goes to the door. A small, intense woman gazes up at him with impatience.

"I'm Santa," the woman says, and then trots in to greet Billy. Dr. Santa Fofana, anthropologist, now retired. Back for the weekend for the sake of nostalgia, something like that.

"Divorce suits you, Billy!" she cries. "You've never looked better!"

"It's Charter here," Billy says. "He has lifted my spirits immeasurably. Come to us from Australia. On a Fulbright. A fan of Loon's."

"Loon!" she erupts with laughter.

Charter feels trapped. How does he justify the harebrained project Billy has so eagerly embraced? Needlessly he explains his Fulbright is *singular*.

"Good for you," Santa says, "to have been *singled out. Loon!*" She laughs disdainfully. This burns him. When Billy goes off to fetch more coffee, Santa makes herself at home among the new cushions. Charter feels compelled to say more.

"There are a few of these, uh, singular grants, ah! Sponsored, I should say, by a family foundation—"

"Is that so?" Santa digs into her purse for a cigarette that Charter is quick to light with the gleaming and somewhat ridiculous lighter Billy keeps on the cocktail table.

"Nadine . . . ," Charter begins. "Nadine Hettering."

"Who?" Santa frowns at him. "Who's this?"

"The Nadine . . . the Nadine Lark Hettering Family Trust."

"What of it?"

"Sponsored—"

"Oh. The Fulbright! Loon! *The Eternal lasts only as long as its aspirations.*" She snorts.

"He's much admired in Australia," Charter says defensively. "Because of his interest, you know, in obscure islands . . ."

"The obscurer the better!" Santa says. Billy hands her a cup of coffee.

"It's fascinating, Santa," Billy says. "Charter lived among the Mannja Fnadr."

"The Mannja Fnadr. Er . . . never heard of them."

"Tell her about the Mannja Fnadr, Charter! Tell her about Noola!"

"God. Where *is* this place?" asks Santa. Billy scurries for the atlas, calling out as he does:

"Sing her the song! There's a *song!*" Billy cries. "Charter knows it!" Charter does all he can to escape, but cannot. He has barely a notion of what he had improvised a week earlier over a supper of shad roe. He is sinking into a nightmare and desperately attempts to come up with something not too ridiculous.

"*Rapa ta runula,*" he begins in a strangled voice, "*Ru nulu oho oho.*" Santa asks what it means.

"Here we stand naked in the breeze—" Charter says.

"Indeed we do," says Santa.

"The Noola is the tree; its leaves, the bird; its beak . . ."

"Hm," Santa exhales. "Where did you say this island is? Any connection to Easter Island? Loon was so taken with Easter Island."

"It is actually quite far from Easter Island," Charter says desperately.

"Well, what isn't?" Santa fixes Charter with two very bright brown eyes.

Charter opens the atlas and points to a spot that is barely there.

"Ah," says Santa. "Rurutu. Its scorpions and its bird gods. Rurutu. A wonderful name, isn't it? It rolls of the tongue like a spoonful of oil. Rurutu! Noola! I want to go to Rurutu," Santa says savagely, "and rub myself down with Noola."

Billy has brought in more coffee and a plate of scones.

"What do they eat on Rurutu?" Santa asks, tearing into one. "Still baking, Billy! Thank god!"

"Ah, well . . . the children—" Charter manages.

"The dear little ones. So cute the little ones. So sad they grow up into cannibals. One wonders why."

"They're not cannibals!" Billy interjects. "Charter says—"

"The hell they're not."

"They. Uh!" Charter thinks his entire upper body is blushing. "They would bring me eggs in little baskets of their making, green leaves and grasses . . . you know. All woven together."

"Oh, I don't know, Charter. Which is why I asked."

"Little blue eggs, rather like quail eggs. I don't recall the names of the birds that lay them. They bake them on coals—"

"Perhaps they were the eggs of the Lulu bird. And the women. Are they perhaps all named Lulu, too, on Rurutu? The men called Roo? I bet my life they all go barefoot, except in the places where the thorny Noola grows."

"The Noola has no thorns," Charter tells her.

"Why not?" Santa asks. "Why not give the Noola thorns?" She smiles companionably as she says this.

Billy, wonderfully amused, chuckles, says:

"The world is a dream, after all! Why not invent all our islands!"

"Oh, but we *do*!" says Santa. "Here's to the Noola and egg eaters of Rurutu, their Lulus and their Randy Roos, too!" She raises what remains of her scone.

"When the islanders have a feast," Billy says gaily, "they slap their bellies like drums."

"Of course they do!" Santa cries. "And I bet they whack the Lulus' bottoms with a nice fat Noola spoon." And then, thank heaven, she stops; Santa and Billy get into recollections of the old days, the people come and gone. When she leaves at last, she says to Charter at the door:

"Next time, Charter, dear, we will have to play cards. I do love to gamble, as I dare say you do, too. We will play Jack of Spades—do you know the game? I do! *I know the game.*" She beams with evident malevolence. "It's a great game for those who know how to bluff." Off she goes into an afternoon as rich in the songs of insects and birds as any island paradise.

—

Charter is so undone he manages to drop any number of things on his way to the kitchen—coffee spoons, an empty dish. But Billy, always in good spirits it seems, does not mind and says only: "I have never seen Santa so playful, so animated! I had no idea she was such a tease. You've charmed her, Charter! I've not played Jack of Spades; you will have to clue me in!" And on and on—Charter, suddenly overcome, runs to the sink and vomits violently onto the small stack of dishes and cups. When he is done Billy gently mops his face and neck with a damp hand towel and insists he lie down. He walks Charter up the stairs, gently patting his back all the way, and helps him into bed. As Charter lies there in a panic, Billy arrives with a glass of ginger ale and sets it fizzing companionably beside him.

Almost at once Charter falls into a deep sleep. He sleeps until the middle of the night, when he is awakened by a nightmare.

He is walking on an island of black lava no larger than the Circle, surrounded by an ocean the color of ink. And Santa is walking beside him, saying:

"You see, there was nothing to your story. Nothing at all. You are naked, young man. As naked as an orange skinned within an inch of its life."

—

Charter lies awake in the lifting dark of early morning, touching his body, prodding his flesh. Slender still, he can feel the start of a belly beneath his hand. His skin is pale, his hair pale, not quite red; freckles are scattered across his nose and cheeks. What little is visible of his beard appears almost white.

As the minutes pass his anxiety increases. He is a lonely child again, his is that foolish name: Stub. The name of a candle burned down to the last inches.

The day his mother left, his father took a hammer to the radio. It was as if he were murdering it. He carried it out back and hurled it to the ground. It bounced. He struck it until it was annihilated. He left the pieces where they lay, so that the backyard became a place neither of them ever wanted to go. The little vegetable garden was abandoned and the flower beds overtaken with brambles. The grass grew, the weeds; soon the sumac took over. The front yard was abandoned and in no time became overloaded with junk. The house was also the place where his father kept the things he thought one day he could make over and sell. Broken toilets, sinks, iron bedposts, and such. He bought a rusted-out truck and used it to haul away whatever people no longer wanted. Stub felt lost submerged in all that broken stuff. He knew that he, too, was not wanted. If it had not been for Axel, the library, the campus, and the woods he thinks he would have fallen to pieces. Like he is now. There is a thread of darkness, a soiled thread, that runs through everything. He is weary and afraid. He lies alone in a borrowed room, adrift. Outside, the world starts up again, but he is somehow excluded from its cohesion. The sound of birds calling up the sun begins.

Soon the Circle is illuminated. A puppy runs around barking. Charter lies in bed barely breathing. If he stands his heart will stop. How will he manage to stand up again? *The world is a riddle,* Vanderloon has written, *an absurd invention we attempt to dignify.* When he smells breakfast he does all he can to pull himself together. When he enters the kitchen, Billy runs to embrace him.

"Feeling better!" he pronounces.

"Billy—" Charter says before taking his place at the table, "I feel such . . . gratitude."

"Now, now my dear boy!" Billy scurries to the refrigerator, but just before he turns away, Charter sees that his eyes are full of tears. The thought of losing Billy makes Charter dizzy with fear. He stares at the table and cannot fathom the bottomless secret of his own existence.

●

After breakfast Charter cuts lilac for the house, and together they fill vases, one for each room. The entire house blooms

with lilac. Then they take a walk together, as they sometimes do.

"You seem to enjoy the quiet life, Charter, as much
as I do," Billy says, pulling up a sweet stalk of grass and
nibbling the broken end. "Were you a solitary boy?"

"Always. I don't know another way to live."

"Concealed?"

"Well, yes, I've always needed to . . . to . . . take cover."

"You and I and Loon. Loon, too, is solitary. When he
retired he vanished. But he never had much to do with this
place—apart from the teaching, that is. Always eccentric.
Bitter. Brilliant, of course. But bitter. Twisted. Well. We are
all twisted, aren't we? More or less." He grabs his nose and
turns it this way and that like a faucet and laughs. The gesture horrifies Charter. "Ah, the fragile children of men,"
says Billy. "Twisted and holy." After a moment he adds: "The
birds do it better than we do."

"Do it?" Charter wonders.

"This business of raising their young. God! The howling that goes on across the way! Maybe Loon is right.
Maybe darkness has more weight—"

"Weight?"

"More . . . authority, persuasion."

"Yes—maybe that is so. How terrible, Billy!"

"We don't have the courage it takes to live in radiance,
when you get down to it. Charter! Why not live in radiance?"

"You do, Billy." Charter looks at him, so close to losing him, with real affection. "If you were a monk sitting

by the side of the road, I believe you'd give your begging bowl away."

—

Charter in Hell. He stands in the shadows gazing into Asthma's window one last time, his mind blazing. One moment he is certain Santa is about to disclose him, call Billy, the Chair, the Fulbright office. The next moment he decides she was teasing him after all. A twisted academic joke. And he wants to set the clock back. He wants to see Asthma as she was, as he *knows her to be*—mercurial, vertiginous, innocent.

A door opens. Asthma and Pea Pod enter the room. A room vivid in the light of a lingering afternoon. They are alone. Goldie and Blackie lie on the grass gleaming with lotion; the Rods are in Goldie's kitchen struggling with a broken Waring blender. Asthma and Pea Pod are moving furniture. Perhaps they are making a little stage. Or a classroom. Asthma the teacher and Pea Pod her pupil. Then it becomes strange. A dream unfolds, the darkest dream. Helpless Charter looks on as Asthma pulls down Pea Pod's panties and smacks her. No, it is impossible! Asthma in the golden afternoon viciously spanking Pea Pod as she stands on a chair, her face in her hands, sobbing.

As then it is over, they are done with the game. It's as if he has seen angels tearing off one another's wings, their limbs as breakable as those of birds. What has he seen? He has seen the end of time. When he turns away from the window, it is as if he has been cut loose; he is unhinged, he is severed from what he has come to count on, what he has come to know. He is thrust out from a deep dreaming that had illumed his path. He sees the far reaches of the world as if from space; any sound takes forever to reach his ears. He is solitary now in new and expected ways. As he falls, he begins to aimlessly wander. The days pass and he is listless. At first Billy supposes Charter has caught the flu and cooks up a large pot of chicken broth. But something else has happened. Something dense has taken over Charter's body, his chest above all, and his head. It is as if heavy bags of sand have been packed into the spaces behind his eyes, between his ribs. *Why,* he wonders, *have the games of children undone me?* He sits for long minutes at a time like an old man in a stupor. He dreams of fog, broken glass strewn across his path. The voices of children stolen and kept under a bell of glass.

"What is it, dear boy?" Billy finally asks after another silent breakfast. "You have not been yourself for days. You drag your feet, and this hound-dog expression . . . Do you miss home? You are so far from your home."

"Billy. Your kindness, always. Yes. Home—I have not been home forever it seems. It will pass. A bit of the blues. I'll take a walk," he says.

"A good way to refresh the mind," Billy approves.

As Charter leaves he pockets a small box of matches. He leaves the Circle forever behind him, descends a brilliantly

green and perfectly shaved hill and walks to the heart of
the campus, making his way to the old painting studio,
weather worn and leaning alone among the trees—maples,
larches. He carries his dislocation like broken wings on
his back, oblivious to the wealth of life in the sky, the trees,
the air.

The studio is ripe with oily rags, cans of turpentine, and
varnish. Dozens of abandoned canvases scaled with paint
are stacked against the walls. As he moves about, particles
of dust race around him. He thinks that at any moment in
the heat of the day the place could combust spontaneously,
something he has read about: a flour mill exploding, a coal
mine, a silo full of hay. He knows so much about so many
things. He is like a sponge, but instead of soaking up water
he soaks up turpentine. He is a cinder in the eye of the
world. He gets down to his filthy business without delay,
then slips out and away, dissolving into the nearby woods
as already the fire cooks up its own weather, its own wind.

Within minutes there is much smoke. The place begins
to pant like a box containing living things struggling to
get out. As the floor swells, pieces of furniture tumble,
collide with the window glass and it happens fast; in no
time, the entire structure heaves, bleeds smoke, and the
flames have reached the second story. A wall falls away
and reveals the Devil's own kitchen—as when Charter was
little and lived in the path of a storm.

In the distance a siren sounds. The fire, he thinks, is
big enough to overcome his confusion. But it isn't. It is

only adding to it. And then he sees Asthma. He sees her leap from a shattered upstairs window. Briefly suspended, her body twists and falls through the air. Leaves spreading beneath her, she hits the high branches of a tree; she tumbles, shouting, from branch to branch, collapsing into the upper reaches and continuing on down, her little cotton dress trailing sparks until, as sirens scour the air, she is snagged. He hesitates. A girl of blood and bone and marrow. His beloved girl broken. And then, her Rod trailing far behind, he sees Blackie, running barefoot down the hill, her terry robe flapping at her knees, shouting Asthma's name over and over. She reaches the tree, the tree that is the only place in the world. The tree that grows at the heart of the world. It is uncanny how Blackie scales it as if she has done this a thousand times. She tears away the dress, she gathers Asthma to her heart, the coveted child, the irreplaceable child madly wanted, saying: *Sweet child. My own daughter. My dearest beloved.* As the fire truck now battles the fire with its mighty powers, an ambulance howls close. There is nothing for him to do but get the hell away and he does, running from the shadows into the deeper woods, the ravine behind, the river beyond, wild in mind with this thing he has done. Asthma. The child who like an angel or bird haunts the high places, the high reaches, and who had come to care for him, to follow him—*the risk of this!* Why had it not occurred to him? A terrible fear overtakes him like a surge of filthy water and he knows he is not fit to live among the many of his kind.

He follows the deer paths, leaps down the familiar rocks, runs mindless of the thorns that cut his face. He runs until he reaches the river, runs along the banks, the beach, runs until he must stop and catch his breath, the ravens complaining everywhere around him. He falls into something like a stupor, stunned, shattered by the inconceivable, and when he wakes it's evening. He washes the blood from his face and arms, and moves on for another hour, perhaps two, guided by the moon. He imagines that she, too, is illuminated in this way, that the moon will heal her, oh, the bright cipher of his heart. He runs again until in the distant dark he sees lights twinkling above him, up on a high embankment. A house, its many windows, the light passing through. He climbs the crest of the hill thick with trees and fallen branches, a richly scabbed-over glacial landscape. Then a path, overgrown, takes him to the house, Victorian, softened to a pearly gray, a driveway that ends in a dirt road that in turn leads to a country road, one of many that wander some distance from the highway. The place is isolated and still. Charter walks, limping a little, up the driveway and stands gazing at the house, its fanciful façade and porch. As he stands uncertain in the moonlight, an old man rises up from behind the railing; he has been sitting in a rocker all this time, silent and hidden from view, watching Charter's approach, his shock of hair startlingly white with eyes of unparalleled intensity.

"Young man," he says, "Are you lost?"

"Yes. Lost! Good evening. I apologize. I fear I may have startled you."

"Where do you need to get to? Come over here! Come into the light."

Charter approaches.

"You are bleeding—"

Inspired by some divine invitation perhaps, Charter says:

"I was hoping to find someone, a reclusive scholar, Verner Vanderloon. I was accosted in the woods—hobos . . ."

"Good *god*!"

"They robbed me, roughed me up. And I have been running and now I have exhausted myself completely. I fear I am in no shape to be seen."

"For godsakes," he says. "And what on earth do you need Vanderloon for?"

"His books! I love his books!"

"Well, you've found him."

"I have?"

"Don't get carried away," Vanderloon says gruffly. "Come. Come inside."

Charter follows him into a beautiful entryway with a long Persian carpet and walls lined with books. He thinks he recognizes a statue from Easter Island, a bird man. As always he notices such things.

"You are badly scratched up," Vanderloon says. "I have some iodine. Come into the kitchen." He takes Charter's elbow and directs him. "So, you like my books. I'd say that is more or less unprecedented."

"Not in Australia!"

"Tomato soup?" Vanderloon reaches for a familiar can. "I imagine you could use some sustenance."

"I *am* hungry."

"Crackers?"

"Yes. Thank you, sir!"

"Loon. Call me Loon. You will have some soup, take a warm bath—I have some salts—and get a good rest. Would you like to stay the night?"

"Thank you!"

"And in the morning you will tell me *just what it is you are wanting.*"

Coffee House Press began as a small letterpress operation in 1972 and has grown into an internationally renowned nonprofit publisher of literary fiction, essay, poetry, and other work that doesn't fit neatly into genre categories.

Coffee House is both a publisher and an arts organization. Through our *Books in Action* program and publications, we've become interdisciplinary collaborators and incubators for new work and audience experiences. Our vision for the future is one where a publisher is a catalyst and connector—between authors and readers, ideas and resources, creativity and community, inspiration and action.

FUNDER ACKNOWLEDGMENTS

Coffee House Press is an internationally renowned independent book publisher and arts nonprofit based in Minneapolis, MN; through its literary publications and *Books in Action* program, Coffee House acts as a catalyst and connector—between authors and readers, ideas and resources, creativity and community, inspiration and action.

Coffee House Press books are made possible through the generous support of grants and donations from corporate giving programs, state and federal support, family foundations, and the many individuals who believe in the transformational power of literature. This activity is made possible by the voters of Minnesota through a Minnesota State Arts Board Operating Support grant, thanks to the legislative appropriation from the arts and cultural heritage fund and a grant from the Wells Fargo Foundation Minnesota. Coffee House also receives major operating support from the Amazon Literary Partnership, the Bush Foundation, the Jerome Foundation, the McKnight Foundation, Target, and the National Endowment for the Arts (NEA). To find out more about how NEA grants impact individuals and communities, visit www.arts.gov.

Coffee House Press receives additional support from the Alexander Family Foundation; the Archer Bondarenko Munificence Fund; the Elmer L. & Eleanor J. Andersen Foundation; the David & Mary Anderson Family Foundation; the Buuck Family Foundation; the Carolyn Foundation; the Dorsey & Whitney Foundation; Dorsey & Whitney LLP; the Knight Foundation; the Matching Grant Program Fund of the Minneapolis Foundation; the Schwab Charitable Fund; Schwegman, Lundberg & Woessner, P.A.; the Scott Family Foundation; the US Bank Foundation; VSA Minnesota for the Metropolitan Regional Arts Council; the Archie D. & Bertha H. Walker Foundation; and the Woessner Freeman Family Foundation.

THE PUBLISHER'S CIRCLE OF
COFFEE HOUSE PRESS

LITERATURE
is not the same thing as
PUBLISHING

The author of eight novels as well as collections of short stories, essays, and poems, Rikki Ducornet has been a finalist for the National Book Critics Circle Award, is a two-time honoree of the Lannan Foundation, and is the recipient of an Academy Award in Literature. Widely published abroad, Ducornet is also a painter who exhibits internationally. She lives in Port Townsend, Washington.

Brightfellow was designed by
Bookmobile Design & Digital Publisher Services.
Text is set in Sabon Next LT Pro.